RECLAIMING HUNTER

STELLA WILLIAMS

SERPENTINE CREATIVE LLC

Contents

Prologue

A glass of 30-year-old scotch in one hand and five shit cards in the other, Hunter Cross dropped a few more chips in the pile at the middle of the table. He should never have let Calix talk him into joining this back-room poker game. Especially when there was much more interesting fun to be had at The Wolf's Den. The Wolf's Den was a run-of-the-mill dance club on the main floor, but a member's only door at the back of the VIP area led to a space where all sorts of debauchery occurred. Anything from back-room business deals to illegal gambling, and of course, space for the more sexually adventurous to play.

Normally, he'd grab a drink and participate in a bit of voyeurism before seeking out a few willing partners for a scene in one of the private rooms. Yet Calix Lupin, one of the club owners, had caught him at the door and offered him a month of free drinks if he took his place at the poker table. Were he and Calix friends? Not in the least, but the man had seemed desperate, so here Hunter was about to lose his shirt, literally. His opponent, Florian Falconer, had the nerve to lick his lips before calling Hunter's bluff.

The move should have pissed Hunter off, but instead, he found himself shifting in his chair. There was no hiding the tent in his boxer briefs. They were playing on a table made of clear resin, specifically made to help deter cheating, however it also made Hunter's desire quite clear. The entire room could see he was hot for the man taking him down ruthlessly in this poker game. They'd lost the other two players; both having chickened out when the game had gone beyond financial gain and moved on to claiming the designer gear they all sported.

Sexual tension hung thick in the air. The room cleared out when it became clear this was becoming more than just a casual game. Giving Florian and Hunter privacy to work out the obvious attraction they both shared. Florian laid his cards on the table, his thick lips curling into a satisfied grin.

"Don't chicken out now, Hunter. Show me what you're working with," Florian teased.

Hunter brought his drink to his lips, taking a long slow sip before tossing down his losing hand.

"You wanna collect here or move to a private room?" Hunter said.

Florian's eyes flashed with desire as he leaned forward.

"Strip."

Hunter's dick pulsed at the command. He stood before slowly lifting his shirt over his head. He tossed the shirt on the table and waited for further instruction. Technically, the rules of the game had been restricted to underwear and not full nude, but that was when others had been in the room. Now it was just the two of them. Hunter had chosen to leave his shirt for last, wanting to see what Florian's reaction would be to the ink crisscrossing his chest and back. It was an homage to his family's legacy of putting logging above all else.

The piece started on his back, a gnarly oak tree whose branches wrapped around to the front of his body, twisting into various animal forms before giving way to storm clouds that swirled low onto his hips and faded into a graveyard on his thighs. In the graveyard were two headstones, one for each of his parents. The tattoo had taken years for him to conceptualize and complete, and he was proud of it, but not everyone got to see the whole thing.

Aside from his tattoo artist, Florian would be the first to see the full piece all at once. If he didn't back out. Florian stood and closed the distance between them, but didn't touch Hunter. Instead, he studied Hunter's tattoo, circling him like he was a statue in some museum.

"You, Hunter Cross, have layers. Who knew?"

"Thanks? I think?"

"Is Calix a friend?"

The question was about their sexual history. As best friends with Calix Lupin, Florian knew damn well he and Hunter didn't associate regularly.

"Not friends, just two people who share similar interests," Hunter said.

Florian stepped closer, the heat emanating from his body searing into Hunter's back.

"Interests?"

"Sex. We both really enjoy sex, and while we've never played together, we've had overlapping circles," Hunter said.

"Overlapping, huh." Florian's tongue swept out to catch Hunter's earlobe.

Hunter hissed and leaned back into Florian. If Hunter thought the nearness of Florian was scorching, the skin to skin contact could melt steel. Speaking of steel, his cock ached with how hard he was just at Florian's teasing. His thin boxers chafed his sensitive flesh as it tried to constrain his engorged length. Hunter had never had this strong of a reaction to anyone before. It was frightening, exhilarating, and he wanted more. It seemed Florian was just as eager to move things along as he reached around to grip Hunter's cock. Florian began to rub him through his boxers; Hunter's hips moved of their own volition, seeking the release he so desperately craved.

"Somebody's impatient," Florian chuckled, releasing him and taking a step back.

Hunter stumbled without Florian there to support him. He tried to course correct but with a not so gentle shove from Florian, Hunter found himself falling into the poker table. Florian was right behind him once again. Hunter silently cursed the thin barrier separating them but doing nothing to hide Florian's own thick cock pressing along Hunter's backside.

"How do you like to play, Hunter? Are you co-ed? Do you play well with others?" Florian rolled his hips.

"All of the above. What about you?" Hunter breathed, pressing back to meet Florian's rolling hips.

"I dabble, but nothing serious," Florian replied.

Florian gripped the back of Hunter's neck and pressed him down hard on the table and continued to rub himself on Hunter. The friction of his rubbing stimulated Hunter's puckered ring. He wanted more, but was afraid to push. This in itself was a game, a game in which Hunter was unsure of the rules, but he knew if he broke even one, it all would come to a devastating end.

Florian closed his eyes and released a slow, controlled breath as his traitorous hips kept grinding against Hunter's ass. Hunter fucking Cross, the one man he had no business pursuing. He'd known it was a set up the moment Hunter had swaggered into the private gaming room. Calix had no doubt noticed the way Florian's attention had been drawn to this particular piece of forbidden fruit and set up this scenario.

Calix Lupin was one of his best friends and saw his attraction as a source of amusement. No matter the history between the Cross Family and both the native and shifter community in the area, Florian's whole being had responded to seeing Hunter at the Wolf's Den for the first time last year. Ever since then, Florian had carefully avoided any interaction with the man, all while keeping a watchful eye. Hunter was hard to miss with his tall muscular frame and red, windswept hair.

Florian hadn't wanted to succumb to another one of Calix's manipulative sex games, but here he was, enjoying only a fraction of what he could with Hunter. The hot logger with the tragic family history, and the boulder on his shoulder to prove it.

It wasn't the first time Calix had tried to set him up with Hunter. There had been the time Calix invited Florian to watch a scene in one of the private play rooms, only to find it wasn't Calix's scene at all. Hunter's head thrown back in ecstasy while being sucked off was one view he'd never forget. Hell, he'd been jealous, not of Hunter's pleasure but of the woman on her knees before him.

Jealousy was new to Florian, but what had made him even more upset was the reaction of his Falcon. His other half had wanted to claw the woman's eyes out for touching what was theirs. The thought of having any claim or ownership of Hunter was enough to have him flee the room and give Hunter Cross the wide berth he had the last few months.

Calix had teased Florian mercilessly about his unwillingness to approach Hunter. So as payback, Florian had bought up three of the properties Calix needed for his arena building plans. He'd held the properties for ransom for months until Calix pointed out Florian's own investments would suffer if Sowell City didn't find another stream of tourist revenue.

That was probably why Calix had felt it safe to set him up once again. Only this time, Florian wasn't sure if there was any payback worthy of this gross overstep by his best friend. Especially now that he'd finally succumbed to his instincts when it came to Hunter Cross.

"I don't think this table is going to hold us both for much longer." Hunter's muffled groan brought Florian out of his mental cave.

Florian had lost himself in thought. He found himself leaning over Hunter's back. The sensual wind of his hips had devolved into manic thrusting, and even the soft silk of his boxers was starting to feel like sandpaper against his sensitized cock. Even worse, he realized his scent mark was somehow seeping through the magic potion Artemis concocted to mask a shifter's mating scent.

"Fuck," he cursed and pulled away. His chest heaved up and down as the panic started to set in. It was one thing to indulge in his lust for Hunter. It was another to leave his scent on Hunter's skin. Any supernatural outside of the Wolf's Den would question his sanity for being involved with a Cross. They wouldn't understand, and it could cost Florian his standing in the community to be linked with Hunter in that way.

"You okay?" Hunter stood and faced him. Concern written clearly on his face.

"I'm fine," Florian bit out, searching the room for his discarded clothing.

"You don't seem fine," Hunter said, crossing his thick, muscular arms over his chest.

The action made Hunter's pecs bulge in a way that made Florian stop in his tracks. His panic was forgotten once again to unfettered lust.

"Can you not look so hot when I'm literally trying to flee from your ass?"

"Why?" Hunter cocked his head to the side, a smug smile spreading across his lips.

"You should know why. You should be trying to flee whatever this is, too."

"I don't run from shit. Otherwise, I would have reneged on my deal with Calix as soon as I saw this was all set up to force us into the same room together."

Florian frowned. "You knew this was a set up the whole time?"

"Yeah, my brain muscles are just as big as the rest of them. I've seen you watching me. I knew you wanted a piece of the fabled Cross action, and to be honest, I've wanted to give it to you from day one."

"You never gave any indication," Florian said. Hunter's revelation threw him so far off balance, he literally sat in one of the empty chairs around the table instead of finishing getting dressed.

"I figured you would make your move when you were ready. Plenty of eager distractions to bide the time with." Hunter's phone buzzed in the pocket of his pants from across the room. Both men looked toward the source of the distraction and then back at each other before the buzzing started again. With a curse, Hunter stalked over to his pants and checked his phone.

"Look, I've got to run, but if you want to try this again, I have a room reserved next week," Hunter said.

Florian should have declined Hunter's offer. Instead, he found himself nodding. "Next week."

CHAPTER 1

Florian clenched his fists so tight his fingernails bit into his skin and drew blood. "You were what?"

He could barely control his anger or the flaring of his mating pheromone as his little sister finished her own angry rant. Vega had just announced over breakfast that she was moving out. Of course, Florian had jumped to the conclusion she only wanted to move out of Sullah and away from him, so she could have male company over. That had pissed her off, and somewhere in her cussing him out, Hunter's name had slipped out of her mouth as an example of her dating someone despite his draconian rules for her and it still ending because of him.

"You heard me! I briefly dated Hunter Cross only to find out I wasn't the first Falconer he'd..."

"He'd what, Vega?" Florian's icy tone belied the raging fires of hell that burned through his insides at the thought of Hunter and his sister together.

Vega was his closest sibling. She knew him better than almost anyone. Knew his temper too, which was probably why she attempted to shift the conversation. "How could you not tell me you were dating Hunter Cross?"

Florian ran a hand through his hair, not caring that it would ruin his carefully gelled pompadour. "Don't try to deflect, Vega."

"We went on a couple of innocent outings. That was all that happened before I found out about you and him. It's why I never mentioned it." Vega's eyes dropped to the floor, and she took a deep breath before her eyes shot back up in accusatory shock. "Is that your mating scent? Are you shitting me right now, Florian? Hunter's your fucking fated mate!"

Florian's biggest secret came pouring from his baby sister's mouth and temporarily distracted him from the fact she had been lying to him. Not only about not dating anyone, but about dating his fated mate. The one man he could never be with because of even more secrets. Florian couldn't talk about this anymore. Not that he wanted to talk about it at all. It had taken him too long to ease the torturous pain of being without his mate. Now to have it thrown in his face that Hunter had gone anywhere near his sister? Too much.

"I don't have time for this, I've got business to attend to," Florian said and left Vega gaping at him as he walked out of the cabin he shared with his fellow Pleasure Pack brother Jacinto.

Jacinto leaned against the railing of the front porch, pretending like he hadn't heard a single thing. Florian knew better, though; the Cougar shifter would have heard every word said between Florian and Vega. To his credit, he at least withheld his commentary until they were halfway to the Alpha's office and well away from other possible eavesdroppers.

"So, Hunter, huh?" Jacinto didn't laugh outright, but Florian recognized the glint of amusement in Jacinto's eyes. His best friend had been teasing him for months about his grouchy behavior, but Florian had managed to keep it somewhat under wraps that Hunter Cross had been the reason for his turbulent moods.

"Shut it," Florian ground out.

"Look, I'm just as pissed as you are that asshole got his hands on Vega, but I also know you've been getting more erratic since you ended things with him. Maybe you should reconsider that non relationship you two had."

"I didn't end anything. There was nothing to end."

"Bullshit! I might not frequent the Wolf's Den, but Calix and his big mouth did enough teasing during those few months for me to know whatever was going on between you was more than your usual fun. Let's not forget the sulking you did when you stopped. It was worse than when you broke up with your last serious boyfriend. Plus, you know I heard everything, right? He's your fated mate, Florian. How long do you think you can keep pretending you're okay without him?"

Florian bit the inside of his cheek. There was no point in trying to hold pretenses with Jacinto. "Even if I wanted to, at this point, I can't. Not after what I did, and not after he's been with Vega, too. Whatever mated madness I fall into is my punishment for even going as far with him as I did."

"You sure they were together like that? Hunter's an immature ass, but he's not that big of a bastard. As much as I hate the Cross family in general, at least this latest generation seems to have some moral coding."

"Whatever there was between Hunter and I, it doesn't matter now. It's been years. Just leave it alone, Jacinto." Florian marched past his best friend and into the Sowell Gate Pack administrative office.

The office was really just an old trailer with the bedroom turned into the Alpha's office. The shelves held rows and rows of handwritten logs containing the history and lineage of the Pack. At least, the most recent ones. The only permanent structure in what was considered the main strip of Sullah was mainly used as storage for older volumes and, occasionally, as a storm shelter for those who didn't have a safe place to stay with Sowell Gates turbulent and unpredictable weather conditions.

Calix Lupin and Aletris Rosen were already there. The Pleasure Pack was all accounted for and present. The main enforcers of the Sowell Gate Pack. Arthur, the official second to the pack Alpha, usually handled the wild Shifters who lived on the mountain, leaving Calix to handle the rest of the Second's duties in Sullah and Sowell City. But once a month, Arthur came down the mountain and took over the role full time for a few days, and they compared notes. Florian checked his watch and frowned. The normally punctual Arthur was late.

"Glad you guys could finally show up. We've gotta hit the trails," Calix said.

"Did something happen?" Jacinto asked.

"Yeah, Arthur got attacked by a rogue bear, and since he is out of commission, guess who gets the pleasure of bringing the rogue in?" Calix said.

Florian shook his head as he registered the dangerous glint in Calix's eyes. Well, not Calix really, but Calix's wolf. Anytime there was a reason to fight, Calix was all in. It made him a good enforcer, but also a bit of a wild card. Thankfully, the rest of the Pleasure Pack balanced out Calix's quick temper. Not that Calix was the most dangerous of the group. That dubious title went to Jacinto. His Cougar would tear anyone to shreds, given the right circumstances.

Jacinto being a Cougar also made it kind of funny that he was the closest to Florian. Florian was a Falcon Shifter. In any other world, their friendship was a nonstarter, yet Florian couldn't imagine having anyone else as his best friend.

"Aletris is going to hang back for this one. We don't want the base camp empty if the rogue is stupid enough to come here," Calix said.

"Lucky dog. I love a good fight, but a rogue bear? The last time we encountered one of those..." Jacinto didn't have to finish the sentence for them to all get the picture. None of them liked to remember that particular fight. They had been young, barely in their teens, and a whole two members stronger as Yarrow had yet to become Alpha and Arin hadn't been sent away by his human family.

"Let's not get in our heads with this one," Florian said.

Reliving that event wouldn't help them in this case. They needed to be sharp and clear of mind. Even with the wisdom of age, Florian wasn't excited about confronting another angry rogue Bear Shifter. He shook off his apprehension and followed Calix and Jacinto out of the office. The three of them loaded up into Calix's SUV, and that should have been the first warning this wasn't just a run-of-the-mill meeting. Calix and Florian had bonded early on with their love of fast and flashy vehicles. The fact that the blacked-out SUV had made an appearance meant, not only were they tracking down this rogue, they were expected to bring them back to the Alpha.

"Something tells me this isn't your typical rogue," Jacinto said as they made their way to Sowell Gate Mountain.

Calix parked the SUV at the end of the road before they took off on foot. "No shifting unless we have to. I think we can all agree we'd rather not take on an angry bear this morning."

Jacinto rolled his eyes and then his shoulders. "That's never been a problem before. You holding out on us, Calix?"

"Maybe." Calix shot them another mischievous grin.

"Better not be anything dangerous," Florian muttered.

"Look, we have the coordinates of the rogue's camp. Let's check that out first, and if things don't look right, we can adjust accordingly."

Calix used his Alpha voice, which meant the time for being buddies was over. They were officially in enforcer mode as they followed Calix's lead up the trails of the mountain and to the rogue's camp. It wasn't lost on Florian just how close the camp was to the Cross family compound. The urge to shift and do a fly over of Hunter's cabin nearly distracted him from the reason he was on this side of the mountains to begin with.

Florian had no idea what he expected when they got there, but definitely not what he saw when they arrived. First thing he noticed were the vehicle tracks; a four runner had been through fairly recently, which meant humans and the human authorities might already be involved. Now it made sense that they hadn't come in their animal forms.

They followed the tracks until they stopped, and Calix cursed. "We've got blood. Human blood."

CHAPTER 2

*B*eep. *Beep. Beep.*

Hunter slammed his fist on his old alarm clock and rolled over. He'd forgotten to turn the damn thing off now that it was the weekend, and it was interrupting the all of five minutes of sleep he'd gotten in the last two days. First, another early blizzard had struck the Cross Logging compound. That meant he'd spent a good amount of energy making sure everything was locked up tight and ready to weather the storm. Not to mention, dealing with the anxiety inducing demands of his Aunt Melinda. Then, having his cousin Baron run off into said blizzard chasing a woman he barely knew, only to be attacked by a fucking bear. To say that Hunter was triggered was an understatement. He'd already lost his father to a bear attack, and more than one other family member maimed. Now, having Baron attacked? Yeah, the Sowell Gate Mountains were the last place you'd ever catch Hunter's ass traipsing around unarmed.

The sun was already shining bright outside his window, and of course, he hadn't closed the curtains last night either. With a groan, he got up and went to shut it tight. He could maybe catch another ten minutes before he was due at the main house for breakfast. He had his own place but didn't see the point of cooking for one when Aunt Melinda always had food enough for an army. A mighty roar sounded outside. He stalled out about a foot away from his window, his heart racing in his chest. Hunter peered outside in time to see a large brown bear running toward the tree line. He rubbed his eyes and looked out the window again.

He could have sworn he'd just seen a fucking bear traipsing by. He shook his head. No way a bear would get this close. Between the people and the noise, there were also plenty of bear deterrents lining the property after what had happened to his father. Then again, a rabid bear like the one that had attacked Baron and his not girlfriend wouldn't care about any of that. Sleep no longer an option, Hunter grabbed some clothes and slid on his favorite boots before pulling his hunting rifle out of its safe. If there was a bear wandering the property, Hunter was about to make sure he scared it off for good, or Uncle Wilhelm would have another piece for his trophy room.

Hunter barely felt the frigid morning air as he followed the bear's paw marks in the snow. At least, it seemed the bear was moving away from the compound. Maybe Hunter was overreacting, but there was no way he was going to let a bear wander around his family. The paw marks disappeared into the tree line, and while Hunter knew he could continue to track it, the loud rumbling of his stomach had him turning back toward the main house. He did, however, want to follow the tracks to see where the bear had gone sniffing around. There wasn't much to attract a bear this far down the mountain. His blood turned to ice as he realized the paw marks tracked almost all the way to Baron's cabin. The real confusing part was about ten feet away, where the tracks turned from bear tracks to human tracks that led all the way up to Baron's porch.

Checking on Baron had been on his to do list anyway, so he shouldered his rifle and stomped up the porch stairs. A heads up for Baron in case he was busy with his woman friend. It didn't seem to matter. After knocking and then letting himself in, Hunter saw that Baron and his friend were not there. Maybe they'd headed over for breakfast already and had totally missed out on their little visitor. He closed the door and made his way down the cleared trail to the main house. The large structure rose into view and, not for the first time, Hunter pondered how much longer the Cross family could go on living in their sheltered little mountain palace. The logging business was booming, but more pressure from environmentalists and the indigenous population of the area was slowly encroaching on their ability to meet demand.

His cousins had made some effort in diversifying the business. Bechet, the younger of his cousins, with reclaimed wood. Braxton, the second oldest, was a gifted carpenter and had added furniture making to the list. Even with the eldest and most traditional of his cousins, Baron, at the helm of the company, it was only a matter of time before the logging aspect of the family business fell to the wayside.

Hunter shook his head as he stomped the snow and mud from his boots before entering the house. What did it matter? Cross logging belonged to his cousins. Hunter was just another cog in the family machine. Spending his time making himself useful wherever he could fit in because it was the least he could do for his aunt and uncle, who had taken him in and raised him as their own. His cousins might not fully appreciate how awesome their parents were, but Hunter did.

He was just hanging his coat when both Bechet and Braxton cornered him.

"You seen Baron?" Braxton asked.

Hunter made a face. "No. I stopped by his place on the way over, but it was empty. I thought he was already over here."

Bechet frowned. "I hope that bastard didn't try to go back up to that campsite."

"With his injuries? He wouldn't be getting out of bed without help," Braxton said.

Hunter shrugged his jacket back on. "Let me check and see if the trail runner is missing. Anyway, not to make this situation worse, but maybe keep the kids and women folk inside today. I saw a bear on the property this morning."

Braxton's eyes bugged out of his head. "You're shitting me," he cursed.

"I wish I was. Damn thing scared the mess out of me this morning. Thankfully, I saw it through my window and not up close and personal. I tracked it to the tree line to make sure it was headed off the property. I'm hoping maybe it just got disoriented in the storm last night and it's not the same bear that attacked Baron," Hunter said.

"See, this is why I spend my time in Mulberry. Won't catch my ass getting mauled by bears and shit in the big city. No offense," Bechet said.

"All offense was meant and taken," Braxton replied.

"Y'all don't start with all that bickering. Let's play it cool until we have more information. Don't want Ma having fainting fits," Hunter said and marched out the door before either of his cousins could reply.

Hunter spent the next hour searching the property for Baron and his girlfriend, Genesis, before hitting the trail up to where he had found them last night. Her camp had been mostly cleared out. Only her tent and the remains of her campfire set up remained. Hunter cursed. Where the hell had they gone? Hunter trudged back down the mountain until he had reception again before attempting to call

Baron for the hundredth time. It went straight to voicemail. Then he checked to see if his cousin had replied to any of the thirty texts he'd sent. Nothing. He was just about to put his phone away when it began to buzz. A call from an unknown number. He normally would ignore it, but with Baron pulling a Houdini act, for all he knew, it could be a hospital or Baron calling from his new girl's phone.

"Hello?"

"Hunter, you need to get to Sullah asap."

Hunter froze mid step, his whole body reacting to the smooth tenor of Florian Falconer's voice. It was a task, but Hunter was able to focus on the anger he felt toward the man instead of the instant butterflies his voice had caused.

"How'd you get this number?"

"My sister, but that's a conversation for another time. Sullah, now, wait at the gate."

The call disconnected, and Hunter nearly crushed his phone in his hands. The nerve of that man. It was the first time they'd spoken in years, and Florian hadn't even attempted to apologize. Hunter was tempted to ignore Florian's demands, but his phone buzzed again. This time with a text from Vega Falconer. Another Falconer he had no business talking to; however, he and Vega had come to form a tense friendship after their awkward break up. Not that it was a real break up. Neither he nor Vega had held any sort of romantic feelings for one another. Impossible for him because he was in love with her brother, and impossible for her because she was in love with her brother's best friend.

V: Sorry not sorry. I gave my brother your number. Seriously though, you need to get to Sullah. I'll meet you at the gate to explain.

H: Why would you give him my number? I'm not showing up.

V: I just did. Get over it. You are coming because your cousin is here.

Fucking Hell, Baron, what are you doing all the way in Sullah!

H: Why is my cousin in Sullah?

V: Just get your ass out here and I'll explain.

H: Fine, I'm on my way, but this better be one damn good explanation

Hunter shoved his phone into his pocket and finished hiking down the mountain, cursing the entire way. If there was ever a place more hostile to the Cross family than Sowell Gate Mountain, the small village of Sullah was it. Hunter may play fast and loose with himself when it came to associating with people from Sullah, but he'd learned his lesson the hard way. Baron was far too responsible to put himself in that type of danger, or at least Hunter believed he had been until recently. This new friend of Baron's was getting to be a bigger pain in the ass than even Baron's ex-wife Christine, and that was saying something.

Florian dusted the dirt off his pants and straightened the neck of his shirt.

"You look fine. Just remember to apologize," Jacinto said.

Florian shot him a dirty look. "I have nothing to apologize for."

"If you really think that, then maybe I should be the one to go talk to him," Vega said.

"Hell no!" Both Florian and Jacinto said at the same time.

Vega didn't even flinch, just rolled her eyes and dusted at Florian's shoulder.

"Neither of you will tell me what happened, but for once, Hunter isn't the bad guy here. Florian, if you want the chance to get Hunter back, you better be nice."

"I may have been wrong to end things, but I had my reasons. How is Hunter not the bad guy?"

"You did something so bad he attempted to date me as revenge."

"Again, how am I the bad guy? And you did actually date him, which you still never explained how that happened," Florian said.

"Don't change the subject. Go tell him what's going on and maybe try to get him to go to coffee or something," Vega pushed.

Jacinto laughed. "Sorry, I just can't picture those two on an actual date. Florian in all his GQ glory, and Hunter in his worn jeans and cowboy hat."

"Hunter doesn't wear cowboy hats. A beanie at most, but only if it's cold. He's as temperamental about his hair as you are," Vega said.

Both Florian and Jacinto looked at Vega.

"One, he has one hat, and he only wears it for special occasions. It's sentimental," Florian said.

What he didn't add was that the hat had once belonged to Hunter's father. One of the few mementos Hunter kept from his old man, who had died in a tragic logging accident involving a rabid bear. At least, that's what the human news had reported. It went without saying that the fact the Bear was a Shifter hadn't been included. Yet another reason he had ended things with Hunter. The Crosses and the Sowell Gate Pack had bad blood that ran longer and deeper than any of the mountain streams.

"Don't start overthinking, Florian. Yarrow is wary of the Cross family, but he's more open minded than past Alphas. Hell, didn't we all just kneel in front of a future Mrs. Cross? He won't hold it against you for pursuing Hunter. Hell, if he truly is your fated mate, no one can hold it against you for following your heart," Jacinto reassured him.

Florian took a deep breath in before slowly releasing it.

"That whole situation is an outlier. I would be willingly walking into this knowing everything," Florian said.

Vega punched Florian's shoulder. "Stop it. That obviously didn't stop you from hooking up with him the first time around. No more excuses. You fucked up and let your mate walk away. Now, go out there and do your best to try to get him back."

Florian scowled at his sister, but squared his shoulders and made his way down the path to the entrance of Sullah. Now that all the ceremonial aspects of the day were over, Florian had nothing better to do than to either waffle with indecision and let his little sister go talk to his mate or he could man up and do it himself.

One last glance back at Vega and Jacinto waving him on before he turned and faced forward. Forward and onward.

Chapter 3

Hunter leaned against his truck, trying to make shapes in the air with his breath. It was cold enough for his breath to be seen, but not nearly as cold as it was in Edgewood on the other side of the mountain. As soon as he'd gotten through the pass, he saw just how much difference the mountain made in the weather. Sullah, while cold, was bone dry, no signs of any snow having fallen on this side of the mountain. Sowell City, which was further into the valley, was probably even warmer than Sullah.

Thinking about the weather didn't do much to aid in Hunter's apprehension about what was to come, but it was much better than letting his imagination run about how and why his cousin had ended up in Sullah. He may joke about the myths and rumors that plagued the region about mysterious animals and Shapeshifters, but Hunter knew the truth. They were real. He'd seen with his own eyes an elderly woman shift into a bear on the mountain. He'd seen the eyes of some of his peers change color and shape when things got exciting. He'd seen Florian's eyes too. The molten gold that glowed in a way that could only be something surreal or magic. All of them had connections to Sullah and the Sowell Gate Mountains.

Even without the myths and legends, the people in Sullah were notoriously closed off with outsiders. They kept to themselves, except for a select few, and by that, he meant the self-proclaimed Pleasure Pack and the Sowell Sisters. That said, the number of reasonable guesses for Baron to be anywhere near Sullah, let alone allowed into Sullah, was limited. The rest was just blind speculation and fantastical ideas.

Hunter had already been cooling his heels for at least an hour outside the gate that blocked outsiders from entering Sullah with their vehicles. He'd rushed all the way here for what seemed like no reason at this point. He was just about to climb back into his truck when he caught movement on the horizon. His heart skipped a beat before the unwanted rush of arousal flooded him. *Florian.*

Unconsciously, he began to straighten, making sure his belt buckle was even before turning to run his hands through his hair a few times, giving it that windswept devil-may-care look. He stopped himself after a moment, shaking his head. He was here because his cousin was in some kind of trouble, and Florian was no one to get all snazzy for. If anything, Hunter should be angry, not flustered. He should spit at the man's feet and cuss him out.

You've already done that, and it didn't make things any better.

The reminder of that night was like adding salt to the gaping wound in his heart. Hunter hadn't planned on falling for Florian. Their whole encounter was just supposed to be a bit of fun. Yet, one time turned into two and then three, and Hunter had realized he wasn't interested in playing around anymore. He wanted the real deal, and with Florian Falconer, of all people. The Fabio of the self-proclaimed Pleasure Pack. Florian always looked like he'd just stepped off a romance novel cover, no matter what the situation.

Today was no exception. As he got closer, Hunter drank in the sight of him. A V-neck tee stretched taut over his pectorals and broad shoulders, and a pair of jeans that were just tight enough to highlight his thick, muscular thighs. The light breeze caught his ebony locks, making them flow and wave as Hunter's fingers rubbed together, remembering how the silky strands had felt in his grip as Florian knelt before him, soft lips wrapped around his cock.

Hunter shifted, adjusting himself in his pants. Now was not the time to be thinking of their brief moments of happiness. Those were long gone. Hunter was madder than a March Hare for even allowing Florian to be such a distraction from the real reason he was there.

He leaned against his truck again, adopting a pose that gave off the vibe he was bored and disinterested. In reality, Hunter fought his body tooth and nail not to reach out and take Florian into his arms as soon as he was within reach.

Florian had the nerve to rake a heated gaze over Hunter before he spoke. "Long time no see, Hunt."

Hunter straightened and shot a glare at Florian. "You don't get to call me that anymore."

Florian scowled right back, but then looked away, rubbing the back of his neck. "That's fair, I guess."

After an awkward moment of them not looking at each other, Hunter broke the silence. "Tell me why I'm here, exactly. You and Vega better not be playing some sick joke on me about my cousin. I don't have the time or the patience. He was seriously injured last night."

Florian's gaze snapped up. There was something dancing in his gaze that Hunter couldn't quite place.

"Your cousin is here, and he's fine. Our healers fixed him up now that he is one of us."

Whatever cocktail of emotions swirling inside Hunter about being face to face with Florian again was replaced with a sense of unease. There had always been rumors about the people who lived in Sullah, not all of them good. Hell, most of them weren't that great. The only thing anyone knew for sure was the people of Sullah had drawn a definite line between themselves and the rest of the Sowell Gate area's population. Especially the Cross family, who they saw as basically the worst colonizers in all of history.

Baron being accepted as one of them wasn't something to spit at. Maybe all the work he and his cousins had done to try to right at least some of the wrongs of their ancestors was finally making some headway. That didn't exactly mean Hunter felt any better about the situation. For all he knew, the help they provided would actually slowly poison Baron to death.

"I don't exactly see Baron coming here to get some help. We got a decent clinic in Edgewood that could have patched him up, and what do you mean he's one of you?" Hunter said.

"Our healers are better. You'll see for yourself in a moment. Your cousin should be coming out soon, so I'm going to try to make this quick. His new girlfriend is from Sullah, and they just finished a commitment ceremony."

"Basically, they just got married in the eyes of your little cult." Hunter held back a laugh.

"It's not a cult."

"Fine, hippie commune, nudist colony, whatever you want to call it."

"Hunter," Florian snapped at him.

"Look, Florian. Thanks for coming out here to let me know my cousin is okay, but I think I'm done with this little forced reunion." Hunter turned to get back into his truck but Florian crowded him against the door, preventing him from opening it. Hunter was bigger than Florian and could have easily overpowered him, but the heat of Florian's body pressed against his back brought back more unwanted memories of raw passion between them.

"I'm not done with you," Florian breathed into his ear before pressing a kiss to the side of Hunter's neck.

Hunter let his head fall back onto Florian's shoulder as he licked and nibbled at the space between Hunter's neck and shoulder.

Fuck, I've missed this. No! Don't fall for his bullshit again.

He pushed hard against the car and used the space he'd created to turn around, putting some distance between himself and Florian. "I'm not doing this with you, Florian."

Florian looked as if he were going to protest or maybe go in for a kiss, Hunter couldn't be sure. Then Florian turned to the side as if he heard something, and Hunter knew that whatever Florian had planned to do, his plans had now changed.

"This isn't over, Hunter. I'm going to call you, and you better not block my number." With that, Florian disappeared into the tree line, leaving Hunter stunned, confused, and pissed the fuck off.

He pulled out his phone and found the unknown number that had called him earlier with every intent to block it. The heat between him and Florian might still be alive and well, but Hunter's willingness to put himself out there like that with Florian had died the moment Florian had made him look the fool that night.

His finger hovered over the block button just a second too long. The sound of giggling brought his eyes up from his phone to see Baron and his new girl approaching. His cousin was just fine alright, and Hunter had it in mind to read him the riot act for scaring the shit out of him.

The happy couple smiled and hung all over each other. And wasn't that just the sight he needed after his encounter with Florian? Hunter pocketed his phone and fixed a smile on his face to hide his sudden jealousy of the happy couple.

Florian watched from the tree line as Hunter greeted his cousin with affection. The bright easy smile he flashed was like a kick in the gut. Hunter had never smiled like that with Florian. Granted, their time together had been limited to hour-long interactions in the private rooms of the Wolf's Den. Florian should never have initiated anything with Hunter to begin with, private or otherwise.

It wasn't like Florian had lacked options when it came to willing bed partners. Yet, he'd walked by at least five of them to get to Hunter that night. Had turned down offers from others to join him and Hunter in the private rooms. Been jealous of the men and women Hunter had entertained during the months before he'd finally made his move. He should have known then that he was on a dangerous path.

He had made the mistake of letting Hunter into his life without realizing the attraction he felt was more than just physical. That the edge he felt whenever Hunter had flirted with others around him was the start of his irrevocable attachment to him. Despite Artemis's advanced knowledge of mating magic, her potion could only mask the scent mark, not make it impossible for his Falcon to imprint on Hunter. If the world were any less cruel, Hunter would never even have been an option as his fated mate.

One thing Florian had always been certain of it was that he would settle down with another Shifter. Falcon Shifters were a dying breed. Even if he had a preference for men, siring offspring was almost mandatory for him. He wasn't even sure Hunter wanted children.

Hell, Florian had thought Hunter was joking when he'd begun hinting at wanting to take their relationship outside the walls of the Wolf's Den.

When Florian realized he wasn't, that was when he'd tried to pull away. He'd avoided Hunter when he saw him at the club. Even began flirting with others in front of Hunter, but that hadn't been enough. Desperate to deny the truth about their relationship, Florian had stupidly pushed Hunter to his breaking point.

Florian closed his eyes, the memory of that night flooding his brain. The anger in Hunter's eyes as Florian had announced his exclusive relationship with another man. He'd hoped Hunter would just walk away, but of course, he hadn't. The resulting confrontation led to Hunter being banned from the Wolf's Den. Being the one place in town where people could freely explore the limits of their sexuality and kink, a ban was basically cutting Hunter off from the one place he could truly be himself.

If Calix hadn't been one of the larger investors at the club, Hunter's ban may have been permanent, but Florian had used up a major favor with his best friend to get the ban reduced to a year instead of forever. Despite the way people still gossiped about the incident, Hunter's reentry into the club last year had been damn near celebrated, and Hunter had seemed to forgive everyone who'd turned on him back then. Everyone, except for Florian.

If Hunter could ever forgive Florian for what happened was yet to be seen. Either way, Florian knew it was going to be an uphill battle to try to win Hunter back. Not just in winning Hunter's trust, but also in trusting Hunter with Florian's biggest secret. Despite Genesis Mabry's blatant flouting of the rules when it came to Baron Cross, bringing a human into the fold was not a small thing. The supernatural world was dangerous for humans in the know. It opened them up to a whole host of situations that could easily go badly for them.

Could Florian really trust Hunter with that knowledge? Florian didn't get long to ponder the answer to that question as his phone buzzed in his pocket. He pulled it out to find a text from Calix.

C: Dude, where are you? We have shit to discuss.

F: On my way.

Florian took one last look, but Hunter and his truck were already out of sight. With a sigh, he turned and headed back into Sullah.

CHAPTER 4

Hunter sat back and watched as his family stared in shock after Baron and his girlfriend/fiancé/cult wife, Genesis, walked out of the room. Aunt Melinda looked about ready to pull another of her fainting spells. Uncle Wilhelm sat next to her, his hands steepled in front of his face in deep concentration. Bechet and his wife, Isis, huddled in the corner and whispered to each other. Hunter couldn't make out exactly what they said, but it probably had to do with preparing to send Baron to some sort of mental health facility and vetting Genesis in case she was a threat to the family and Isis's political aspirations. Braxton's wife, Carmen, rocked a sleeping Brayden while Braxton stared at them in the kind of wonder only a man in love could.

Yet, everyone seemed to be oblivious to the big picture. Hunter seemed the only one who understood that while the rest of them had been worried about Baron's wellbeing, only Genesis had truly helped him the way he needed. If that wasn't the biggest sign that maybe Baron wasn't as crazy as everyone thought when he said he was in love, then Hunter didn't know what was.

"Well, I'm headed in for the night. I don't know about y'all, but it's been an exhausting few days." He stood and walked out of the house before anyone could stop him. Not that they had tried. They were all caught up in whatever they were thinking and doing.

On his way to his cabin, Hunter kept a lookout for bear tracks. He doubted the bear would return to the scene of the crime during the day, but walking alone, he wanted to be careful. It would be just his luck that he would meet the same fate as his father. Caught off guard by a rabid bear while minding his own business.

An extra shiver ran down Hunter's back. The feeling of being watched was unmistakable. He looked over his shoulder a few times and gave the tree line a hard once over, but there was nothing he could see in any direction. Then a shadow passed over his head, and he looked up in time to see a large bird fly by. He took a second to follow its flight path, admiring the ease with which it floated above. Its large wings flapped just enough to keep it alight in the icy wind. It circled and swooped close enough that not only was Hunter able to identify it as a Falcon, but he could feel the tiny gusts of wind caused by the flapping of its wings. They tickled his face almost like a lover's caress. Shaking his head, Hunter tramped the rest of his way to his cabin.

His run in with Florian was really throwing him for a loop. The Falcon was probably hunting for an easy meal, as small rodents would come in droves to be near the warmer houses. Speaking of, Hunter headed to his small kitchen to make sure his snack pantry hadn't become home to some of those same critters while he'd been traipsing back and forth from the main house. While he was in there, he snagged a box of Fruity O's and dug in. The crunchy sugar cereal was his idea of comfort food.

Growing up with a single father who spent more time worrying about chopping down trees than chopping vegetables meant Hunter had relied on easy to make meals and his Aunt Melinda's pity to feed himself. Hunter's mother had died in a car accident when he was a toddler. She'd gone to Sowell City to shop and on her way home, a freak storm had caused a rock slide. Unconsciously, he rubbed his thigh where the tattoo of her gravestone lay.

Hunter shoved another handful of cereal into his mouth and flopped down on his coach. He flipped through his DVR, finding the perfect thing to get his mind off his family and personal drama. The young chairman swapped the bell pepper for an apple and took a giant bite. The American reboot wasn't nearly as entertaining as the classic Japanese cooking show, but Hunter's brain was too tired for subtitles.

They were just about to reveal the secret ingredient when Hunter's phone buzzed. He wanted to ignore it, but with everything going on he couldn't in good conscience fully retreat from it all. As much as Hunter liked to play with everyone's idea of him being the carefree ne'er-do-well, in reality, he was the exact opposite.

He set down his snack and pulled out the offending object, praying it was something he could ignore and get back to relaxing. His scowl deepened when he saw it was the same unknown number that had called that morning. Florian's number. He was two seconds from sending the call to voicemail and blocking the number when the buzzing stopped and a message came through.

Unknown: You can't avoid me forever

Hunter: You wanna bet

Unknown: You should know by now I never bluff

Hunter: Goodbye, Florian

After sending the text, Hunter blocked the number. There was nothing he wanted to talk about with Florian, and no good could come from entertaining the idea they could ever be friends or any such nonsense.

Florian was pretty sure Hunter had blocked his number after the third message went unanswered. With a curse, he tossed his phone to the side. So, the heat between them was obviously still there; this afternoon while pressed against Hunter's back Florian had felt it. The racing of Hunter's heart, the way his muscles relaxed into his. Yeah, Hunter's body knew exactly where it belonged. If only Florian could figure out a way to get Hunter to allow him the time to convince his mind as well.

Messages and calls weren't getting him anywhere. Making flights over the Cross Logging Compound wasn't going to help things either. It was only a matter of time before his clandestine spying got him in serious trouble with the Alpha. That side of Sowell Gate was Coven territory, and he had not gotten permission from the Head of the Coven to be in the area.

A soft knock on his bedroom door startled him. "What?" he called.

The door opened, revealing Jacinto dressed in a sweater and a pair of chinos.

"Hey! Just letting you know I'm headed out for the evening."

"Hot date," Florian teased.

Jacinto rubbed the back of his neck and shook his head. "You know, it's my aunt's birthday today."

Florian laughed, "Right, you should probably change clothes then. You know damn well she's not having some tame dinner party."

"Actually, the first half is a dinner party. My cousin Zahina insisted on that before Aunty gets too turnt up, as she would say."

Florian shook his head.

"If anyone should be getting turnt up, it's you. I swear, man, it's like these last two years you've lost your mojo."

Jacinto squinted at Florian.

"We both know you have enough mojo for the both of us, despite us being in the same position."

Florian nodded solemnly. "You still haven't told me who your mate is, and I find that extremely unfair."

"Well, suck it up, buttercup, and no flybys on Hunter tonight. You really need to see the Coven Master first."

Florian flicked off his best friend, who smirked and left. Jacinto wasn't wrong. Florian needed to get permission to be in Coven territory so frequently as not to threaten the centuries long treaty between the Sowell Gate Coven and the Sowell Gate Pack. He picked up his phone and sent a text to Artemis. She was the only person he trusted not to disclose this private venture of his. Hell, she'd helped him and the others mask their mating scent for years. She'd probably be happy not to have to waste her energy with him anymore.

"What?" Artemis's sharp tone snapped at all of Florian's nerve endings.

"Sorry to disturb you so late, but I need a favor."

"I don't do favors," Artemis reminded him.

"You can name your price," Florian said.

"This better not be any bullshit, calling me this late."

"It isn't. I need a meeting with the Coven Master."

There was silence on the other end for what seemed like an eternity.

"And why would you need that?"

Florian fiddled with the edge of his bed sheet, unsure of how much he should reveal to Artemis. She was shrewd and not a gossip, but she was one of Vega's best friends. He didn't need her running her mouth to his little sister about any of this. Even if it was partly Vega's urging that had brought him to this point.

"I need permission to enter Coven territory to court my mate," Florian breathed out.

Again, there was silence before the impossible happened. Artemis laughed. Not the snide snickering or rude guffaw she was known for, but a full laugh that rang out like a cacophony of tinkling bells with a melody so sweet Florian couldn't help but smile.

Then the laughter stopped, and Artemis cleared her throat. "You didn't hear that, but you will hear from me at an appropriate time of day about this meeting."

With that Artemis hung up, leaving Florian feeling both relieved and petrified. If Artemis succeeded in securing the meeting, Florian would have to notify Yarrow of his plans. Yarrow Lupin was a chill guy and a fair Alpha, but bringing another Cross into the fold so soon might be too much even for him to accept. Not because Yarrow would deny Florian his true mate, but the reaction of the rest of the Pack might not be as favorable in the end. This, on top of having to somehow convince Hunter to give him another chance. Florian hadn't quite figured that part out yet, but he figured the more red tape he could cut through on his end, the clearer the path for him to prove to Hunter how serious he was about him.

CHAPTER 5

Hunter took a sip of his black coffee, eying Vega suspiciously as she nibbled on her lemon blueberry tart. It wouldn't be the first time they'd met at Flower Cafe for coffee, but given recent events, Hunter was skeptical about Vega's motives.

"Quit glaring at me, Hunter. I gave Florian your number because it was important," she sighed.

"You didn't just give him my number, you ambushed me," Hunter snarled.

Vega shrugged and sipped her lavender latte.

"That wasn't part of the plan. Florian insisted, and Jacinto, well, he was very persuasive."

Hunter rolled his eyes. "Why don't you stop meddling with me and Florian and focus on Jacinto instead?"

Vega's eyes widened. "Shh, don't say that so loud."

"Ain't nobody paying us any mind. Anyway, I'd appreciate it if you dropped this whole matchmaking scheme you seemed to have cooked up overnight. Nothing will ever happen between Florian and I, just like nothing ever happened between us two," Hunter said.

"It's not my scheme. I mean, I'm totally rooting for you and Florian to hook up, but I understand things are complicated. Trust me, I understand. Anyway, I just wanted to warn you that Florian has made his intentions toward you clear to the leadership and elders of our community. He will make a concerted effort to court you, and if there is any chance you can forgive him for what he did the first time around, please try."

Hunter sat back in his chair. Of all the things that could have come out of Vega's mouth, that was the last thing he'd expected or even wanted to hear. "I don't give two shits about who he's told or what his intentions are. What we had is dead and has been for a long time now."

Vega sighed and finished her tart before downing the last of her latte. "Fine, be stubborn about it, but seriously stop hating him, at least. It's been years."

Hunter toyed with the edge of his napkin, not able to look her in the eyes as he pondered giving up the anger he'd clung to for the last few years. Shaking his head, he said, "If I stop hating him, I'll love him, and I can't keep doing that either. Now, can we change the subject?"

Vega gave him a pitying look and took his hand in hers. "I just wanted to give you a heads up as your friend."

"You sure you're my friend in all of this?"

Now it was Vega's turn to glare at him. "Don't shoot the messenger, Hunter. We should get going if we want to make our appointment with the Hancocks."

Hunter downed his coffee and nodded. Vega was one fourth of the Sowell Sisters, and Sowell Sisters Boutique and Events was Sowell City's first one stop shop event planning agency. Landing the contract for the Hancocks' annual spring soiree would put them on the map. The Hancocks, the Buchanons, and the Crosses were the first European settlers in the Sowell Gate region, and while the Crosses fancied themselves to be followers of the pioneer spirit, the Hancocks and the Buchanons were definitely more like his Aunt Melinda's family. Aristocrats who liked to flaunt their family wealth and historical standing within the area. Hunter had been forced to attend their soirees more than once with Aunt Melinda, but now he would use his tenuous connection with the family to help Vega with her new company.

"Hunter, darling. It's so good to see you," Candice "Candi" Hancock said, giving Hunter a hug that lasted just a tad longer than appropriate.

"Nice to see you too, Mrs. Hancock," he said, putting emphasis on the Mrs.

She stepped back and swatted playfully at his shoulder. "Oh, Hunter, please. How many times have I told you to call me Candi?"

"Sorry, Mrs. Hancock. My aunt would have my hide if I didn't abide by the rules she raised me with," Hunter said, pasting on a sheepish grin.

"Good morning, Mrs. Hancock," Vega said, making her presence known.

Mrs. Hancock's playful manner evaporated as she studied Vega, who stood next to Hunter. The look of disapproval on Mrs. Hancock's face was enough to tell Hunter this business venture would be an uphill battle. Possibly would have been a nonstarter if Hunter wasn't offering his support.

"I do hope it shall be a good morning, Ms. Falconer. I've had Milly set up tea on the terrace for our chat," Mrs. Hancock said.

"That sounds lovely," Vega said, and they both followed Mrs. Hancock to the back terrace.

Hunter sat and watched as Vega did her magic. Mrs. Hancock may have been apprehensive about working with someone from Sullah, but Vega's natural charm and professionalism quickly won over Mrs. Hancock. No sooner had Mrs. Hancock seen the first vision boards for the event before she was oohing and awing and talking excitedly about working with Vega and the Sowell Sisters. Hunter's presence was all but forgotten until Vega's presentation wrapped up and a second appointment was scheduled to finalize details.

"So, Hunter, are you planning to bring a date or shall I have Milly on hand to chase you out of dark corners again this year?" Mrs. Hancock said as she escorted them back to the front door.

Hunter chuckled and glanced over at Vega, who had an amused and calculating look on her face. "Don't trouble Milly with me on one of her few nights off. I promise to be on my best behavior, date or no date."

Mrs. Hancock laughed, "I won't hold you to that."

Hunter walked Vega to her car first, wanting to see her on her way before going to his own truck. "Don't get any crazy ideas about setting me up, Vega."

Vega smiled brightly. "Who me? I told you I don't plan to interfere with your dating life."

With a wink, she slid into her car, and he closed the door behind her. Shaking his head, he knew while she might not directly interfere, that didn't mean she wouldn't get her crazy friends involved. This whole morning felt like one long ploy to test out Hunter's feelings about Florian, and as much as Hunter didn't want to admit it, part of him was excited to hear Florian was, in fact, interested. The fact had zero bearing on Hunter being receptive to reconciliation. He wasn't at all interested in that part, but after yesterday's encounter, Hunter would have been lying if he said he wasn't tempted to reexamine his physical connection to Florian.

Florian tightly gripped the wheel of his Ferrari as he guided the electric blue beauty through the pass on his way to his meeting with the Sowell Gate Coven Master. The sleek, flashy vehicle was probably not the best choice for the trip, but he just couldn't resist the temptation of the road's sharp winding curves. The purr of the engine, the excitement of his excessive speed, the utter focus required to navigate the mountain road without flying off a cliff were just barely enough to distract Florian from the rapid firing of his nervous system. He was actually doing this. He was really going to stake his claim on Hunter Cross.

Florian's meeting with Yarrow that morning had been brief and terse. He'd been right about Yarrow's lack of enthusiasm over Florian's revelation that Hunter was his fated mate. He and his mate Amayah had both seemed shocked and apprehensive, to put it nicely. However, fated mates could not be kept apart by Shifter law. Even if he truly was against the union, there was nothing Yarrow could do about the situation any more than Florian could.

The soft trill of Florian's phone nearly broke his concentration in the middle of a rather precarious curve. It was only Florian's deft handling and the vehicle's impeccable responsiveness that kept him safely on the paved route. With a curse, he hit the answer button conveniently located on the front of the steering wheel.

"Yes, my dearest Vega." There was no hiding the sarcasm in his tone, even if he wanted to.

"I'm going to ignore your attitude this morning only because I know it's not really about me. Anyway, guess who I just met with?"

"Who?"

"Mrs. Hancock!" Vega squealed.

Florian grit his teeth as the high-pitched noise came out of his speakers and stabbed at his eardrums.

"That's exciting?"

"Why yes, dear brother, it is. For one, landing this contract with Mrs. Hancock for her spring soiree will cement Sowell Sisters Boutique and Events as the place to go for party planning in the Sowell Gate Area. Two, my meeting revealed some interesting information that you might want to know."

Florian doubted there was anything about Candi Hancock even remotely important to him, but he decided to play along. Humoring his baby sister was a much better distraction than driving recklessly through the mountain pass.

"And whatever could that be?"

"So, I have Hunter to thank for introducing me to Mrs. Hancock in the first place, so it was only right that he accompany me on our first meeting."

"You saw Hunter!"

So much for a distracting conversation. Just the thought of Hunter and Vega being anywhere together grated him harder than a block of Parmesan cheese.

"Let me finish before you get all agro over your mate, who I remind you I only fake dated."

Her reassurance did nothing to quiet the jealous rage he felt, but he bit down hard to keep from saying anything else until she was done.

"Anyway, Hunter was there for support, and Mrs. Hancock brought up that Hunter doesn't usually come to her event with a date. I thought that if everything goes okay with Yarrow about the whole mating a Cross thing, that maybe you could find a way to be Hunter's date for the evening."

Unconsciously, Florian's grip on the steering wheel relaxed and his teeth unclenched. There was nothing he could do about his runaway nervous system, but at least he wasn't about to claw up his precious leather interior in a fit of rejected mate rage.

"Thank you for the information and the vote of confidence. I had a chat with Yarrow this morning, and while he is hesitant about the situation, he isn't against it. Anyway, I hope you get the contract for the event. I don't say this enough, but I really am proud of you, my little vegetable."

"Ugh, don't call me that, but thank you and you should say it more often. Now, I can hear that you are driving, so I'll let you go, but we are definitely discussing this more over dinner tonight. You need a good plan of attack."

Florian smiled and shook his head. Vega had always been his favorite sibling and not just because they were the closest in age, but because, unlike their older siblings, Vega had always had his back.

"Goodbye, Vega."

He ended the call before she could press him further about dinner and his plan of attack, as she put it. Florian knew well that winning back Hunter's affection would be very much akin to war, but he hoped it would be a short one. The rest of the drive into Edgewood went by almost peacefully as the rugged mountains gave way to a lush forest scape. Edgewood was tucked away behind a wall of green, built in what was basically a massive clearing. Florian quickly found the only diner in the one road town and parked out front.

Edgewood wasn't big on outsiders, but they also would not turn down a paying customer, so he ordered the least offensive looking thing on the diner menu and waited patiently for Ambrose to arrive. The last thing he expected was for Genesis to slide into the booth across from him a few minutes later.

"Hey Flor! What brings you to this side of town?"

Florian scowled, but immediately fixed his face into a nonchalant smile. "I've heard this place has amazing milkshakes."

Genesis' eyes lit up, and she nodded enthusiastically. "I've heard the same, which is why I'm here. I rarely pass up on a chance to exercise my sweet tooth. I'm getting mine to go, but since you are here, I'd like to ask a favor of you."

Florian didn't know what she was going to ask, but he was pretty sure he would not be willing. He didn't know Genesis; she was a mystery, and he absolutely hated the jovial optimism she seemed to exude even when faced with the shit storm that was her rise to being the Pack Beta. Still, she was the Beta, and he had sworn to follow her guidance, at least in Pack matters, so he simply nodded and motioned for her to continue.

"I need a mentor. I'm new to all of this," she paused and glanced around before lowering her voice and leaning slightly forward, "Pack business."

"Obviously. Would you like me to set you up with one of the elders?"

Genesis sighed and sat back. "No, I was hoping you would help me. Yarrow mentioned in his call this morning that you would be on this side of the mountain more frequently because of your mate and that you might need something to fill in your downtime between courting."

If there was ever a point in his life where he felt the urge to challenge the Alpha, it was right at that moment. "Did Yarrow mention who my mate was?"

Genesis shrugged, "No, but um, I did catch a vibe between you and Hunter."

"You've never seen me with him," Florian said suspiciously.

"No, but I caught a scent when walking with Baron and was surprised it was all over Hunter when he came to pick us up. I didn't know it was your scent then, but it wasn't hard to figure out once Baron told me the rumors about the little triangle he had with you and your sister."

"Vega and Hunter were never—" Florian rose from the booth in his growing ire but quickly sat back down. "Sorry," he muttered.

"It's okay, I get it, but truthfully, this situation could work out for both of us. I would get your expertise about Shifter stuff and you'd have a legit excuse to have casual run-ins with Hunter."

Florian chewed on the inside of his cheek. A habit he'd thought he'd broken in middle school. He forced himself to stop and take a deep breath. "Fine, I'll do it, but you must not interfere with my courtship of Hunter."

"I wouldn't dream of it."

"Then it's a deal. Now, if you don't mind, I'm waiting for someone," Florian said.

Genesis nodded before grabbing a napkin and producing a pen before scribbling down her number and sliding it over to him. "So you know how to reach me. I'll also have Baron clear you to go beyond the public area of the estate and up to the compound."

With that, Genesis slid out of the booth, and it was just in time, as Ambrose, the Coven Master, came striding into the diner. The man's energy couldn't be contained. It filled the air with an electricity that snapped and crackled along every one of Florian's nerve endings. He could tell Genesis felt it too as she eyed Ambrose with curiosity before accepting her order from the young waitress behind the counter.

"Florian Falconer, the last man I thought I'd ever be having an audience with," Ambrose said gleefully as he slid into Genesis's abandoned spot.

"It's good to see you too, Ambrose. I see Daddy's robes are settling nicely on you." "See, this is why I like you. You don't let some silly facts like my ability to totally wreck your plans get in the way of your snark."

"On that subject, I'm here to ask your permission to enter your territory more frequently than is agreed upon in the current treaty."

"Yeah, Artemis filled me in. Has it really gotten that bad over on the other side of the mountain? Y'all are smashing Crosses like bored teens smashing pumpkins on Hallows Eve."

"Wow, way to be inappropriate in the first," Florian made a show of checking his watch, "three minutes of talking."

"Look, I'm only kidding, sort of. I'll allow you leeway for courtship, but make sure it's clear to Yarrow I'm not looking to house half your family just because dating sucks over there."

"I'll be sure to relay the message. Thank you for being somewhat reasonable about this."

Ambrose let out a deep bellied laugh that drew the stares of the few people eating around them. "Dude, honestly. I'm going to enjoy watching this shit show in the making."

Florian really wanted to punch Ambrose in the face, but that would be saved for when Ambrose made his trip into Sowell City to wet his prick outside of the Coven coffers. For now, Florian reached for his wallet and dropped a few bills on the table to cover the food he'd ordered but still hadn't received. "As always, thank you for the tiresome companionship."

He was treading a dangerous line with this meeting and his attitude, but Florian didn't care as long as he got the permission he needed to start on his plan to win Hunter back. Now that the outside forces keeping them apart had been handled, he could work on the bigger issue. Getting Hunter to trust him again. It wasn't going to be an easy task, but Florian was confident that since he'd so easily won Hunter's trust in the past, this time wouldn't be too hard either.

CHAPTER 6

Hunter's eyes bugged out of his head when he rounded the corner and came face to bare chest with the last person Hunter would have ever expected to be allowed on the Cross family compound. Yet this wasn't his first time seeing Florian. For the last week or so, he'd caught glimpses. Fleeting glances of Florian just around the corner, there but then gone. Hunter thought he'd been losing his mind. Now he was certain this had to be some kind of mistake. Some sick joke by one of his meddling kin.

"What the fuck are you still doing here?" he barked before he could reel in his anger.

Florian had the nerve to grin ear to ear as his gaze swept up and down Hunter's frame. Hunter's scowl deepened as his body reacted to Florian checking him out, every tingle, all the heat, particularly the tightness in his jeans as his traitorous body continued to ignore the signals from his brain to hate Florian with every fiber of his being.

"Oh, hey Hunter!" Genesis said, coming out of Baron's cabin in a pair of leggings and a sports bra, despite the nippy temperatures of early winter.

Hunter glared at his cousin's fiancé. "You invited him here?"

Genesis cocked her head to the side and frowned. "Yeah, that a problem?"

"It's a big problem," Hunter hissed.

She shook her head and patted Hunter on the shoulder. "Well, he is my invited guest. You, on the other hand, were not invited to my training session, so if you don't mind." Genesis moved past Hunter and signaled for Florian to follow her away from Baron's and toward the open space between the house and the tree line. Hunter was pissed, but he couldn't stop himself from watching as both Florian and Genesis sunk into a fighting stance. With a simple nod from Florian, Genesis launched forward on the attack. Florian expertly dodged her charge and her flying fists before sweeping his leg out and sending Genesis falling flat on her back.

Genesis angrily pushed herself off the ground while Florian stood smirking above her, his long hair swinging in the single braid he'd tied it into. Hunter couldn't hear what they said, but it didn't matter. He was too stuck in his memories of Florian's graceful body hovering over his, the way his ab muscles rippled with every thrust. Hunter closed his eyes. Two years of keeping his distance, a year of being exiled from one of the few safe spaces in town, and he still couldn't forget the fun they'd had together. Still couldn't forget the immense pleasure they shared in the back rooms at the Den. Yet, he also wouldn't let himself forget when it all came crashing down.

"You alright, bro?"

Hunter opened his eyes to see Baron holding a steaming cup of coffee in one hand and the morning paper in the other.

"Uh yeah, I was just stopping by so we could chat about the Markham property," Hunter said, remembering why he'd been headed to Baron's cabin in the first place.

Baron frowned. "Shouldn't you be looking for Braxton or calling Bechet for that?"

"Any other time, yes, but Old Paul specifically requested that you come and ask for permission to tear down that old barn of his. Says he'll only talk to the boss."

With a curse, Baron set his coffee down on the railing of his porch. "I'm sure that went over swell with Bechet."

Hunter chuckled at that. "He was a little hot under the collar, but you know Bechet's always willing to put business before personal issues. So, whatdayasay? Wanna head over with me today or am I breaking the news to Bechet that my latest source of reclaimed Cross lumber has backed out?"

"Nah, I'll tag along. Just let me tell Genesis I'm headed out?"

"What? She's got you whipped already?"

Baron ignored his jab and headed to where Genesis and Florian had continued their sparring. Hunter watched as Baron chatted briefly with Genesis before the new couple shared an obscenely passionate kiss. Florian averted his gaze from the couple, only for it to land on Hunter. For a moment, Hunter swore he saw a flash of gold in Florian's eyes before he blushed and looked away. Another reminder of why Hunter should stay away from Florian Falconer.

While the rest of what was considered the sane part of the Cross family didn't believe in the rumors about Shapeshifters in the area, Hunter was a believer. He'd had too many strange encounters not to believe. Yet, he could only speculate that Florian and Vega were more than who they portrayed themselves to be. Hunter refused to let himself fall down the rabbit hole of the local lore at the moment. He pulled out his phone and made a show of checking the time, all while taking a stealthy photograph of Florian's half naked torso.

Not wanting a relationship with the man didn't mean Hunter couldn't enjoy looking at him when he dangled his body in front of him like the forbidden fruit it was. After snapping enough pictures to satisfy his lustful curiosity, Hunter really did check the time and curse. Baron and Genesis still hadn't come up for air, and he did not have time for any of this. Markham was waiting on them, and Hunter didn't want to piss the old man off before they even got to haggling over pricing.

Hunter wasn't the only one growing impatient with the new couple. Florian had apparently run out of options to look at to avoid looking at Hunter, and shit, now he was coming Hunter's way. With purposeful strides, Florian closed the distance between them. Hunter could not tear his gaze away, holding Florian's stare as the familiar heat of arousal spread through his body and concentrated at his groin.

"What do you want?" Hunter growled, holding out his hand to keep Florian from getting any closer.

Florian took another step, pressing his chest into Hunter's hand.

"Just checking something," Florian replied.

Hunter made a face. "Checking what?"

Florian wrapped his hand around Hunter's before taking another step. Hunter's stiff arm relaxed, allowing Florian closer and closer until his bare chest pressed into Hunter's, their hands caught between them. Hunter could feel Florian's heartbeat speeding up the closer they got to each other, just like Hunter was sure Florian could feel his now that the distance between them was practically nil.

With a smirk, Florian leaned in, Hunter tilted his head in preparation for his lips to press into his only for Florian to deviate from the path. His lips brushing delicately along Hunter's cheek before Florian whispered in his ear, "Yeah, you still want this."

The cocky arrogance of Florian's tone should have snapped Hunter back into his senses, but instead, he found himself smiling against Florian's cheek.

"Sexual attraction was never the problem, Flor. You were," Hunter said before pushing Florian away.

It was just in time as, at last, the other couple wrapped things up and Baron headed back Hunter's way with a new pep in his step.

"We'll talk again, soon," Florian said before jogging back to where Genesis eyed them with laughter in her eyes.

Baron looked between Hunter and Florian and shook his head. "You sure you want to bark up that tree again?" he asked, ever the concerned older cousin.

"You got any spit left in your body after that little slob show?" Hunter teased, nudging Baron in his ribs.

The last thing Hunter wanted to talk about was Florian, and teasing Baron about his new whirlwind relationship would surely distract his lovestruck cousin from the topic. Hunter wouldn't admit it out loud, but he truly did envy his cousin for the relationship he had with Genesis. Sure, it was new, and rushed would be a generous term for their courtship. It had barely been a week from when they first met and when they got engaged. Yet, it was clear the difference she made in his broody older cousin's life, even in just the month she'd been around since.

The first and only time Hunter had ever felt anything even touching that kind of thing had been his time with Florian and, well, he was done thinking about that. He was done thinking about Florian. If Florian was going to be around to help Genesis with whatever the fuck it was they were doing, maybe this was the universe's way of forcing him to let that shit go.

"Don't be jealous. You want me to wait while you get a little extra dose of joy from your boyfriend?" Baron replied.

Hunter scowled. So much for changing the subject. Baron had just escalated Florian from sketchy ex to boyfriend. Something Florian had never been. "Florian isn't my anything."

Baron smirked. "Maybe not right now, but he obviously isn't over whatever you two had going before, and from the looks of things, neither are you."

"You have no idea what you are talking about," Hunter grumbled, sliding into the driver's seat of his truck.

Baron climbed into the passenger seat and buckled up.

"So, why don't you tell me and without all the bullshit machismo?"

"Ain't nothing to talk about. We had a meaningless fling. It ended."

"It doesn't seem like it meant nothing."

"How would you even know?"

"I'm assuming you aren't blind as shit and see the way that man looks at you?"

"All because he wants my sexy ass body doesn't mean he wants anything more. Been there, done that, got the scars to prove it."

"You telling me he hurt you? Like, physically hurt you?"

Hunter chuckled and shook his head. "Not without proper consent, but that's a different story. Anyway, just leave it alone. If he's on the property to help Genesis, then fine, but keep him away from me."

"You sure that's what you want? Didn't seem like it the way you two were sharing air back there," Baron said.

"Look, just because you found a second chance at happily ever after with Genesis, doesn't mean Florian deserves a second chance with me," Hunter said, flustered by his cousin's insistence that Hunter examine his current choice to keep Florian at arm's length.

Baron shook his head and rubbed a hand over his face. "If you're one hundred percent sure there is no coming back from whatever happened, then so be it. I'll try to keep Genesis's matchmaking schemes to a minimum then. Just promise me you will stop with the angry drunk act. Heartbroken and full of regret doesn't look good on anyone. Trust me, I know from experience."

"I'll try." Hunter sighed with relief that he didn't have to explain in detail just how much Florian had hurt him. Even if Baron had wanted to continue that line of conversation, they had arrived at the old Markham farm. It wasn't much of a farm now. About thirty years ago, it had been converted to a ski lodge, but the locals hadn't liked the tourists tramping around and disturbing the peace of the trails. That, and a few random animal attacks had closed the lodge up for good about twenty years ago. Now it was more or less an overgrown piece of land quickly being reclaimed by the Sowell Gate Forest.

Torey Markham stood in front of the entrance of the lodge, looking like he would rather be anywhere else. Hunter couldn't blame him. The Markhams and the Crosses had a similar family history with the animals on the mountain. The history? A long line of unprovoked attacks that left them either dead or seriously maimed. The difference, the Crosses had buckled down and stayed while the newer generation of Markhams tucked tail and ran. Not just from the mountains, but the state. Relocating to the bright lights and skyscrapers of Mulberry.

"Hey, Torey! Thanks for reaching out!" Hunter said, coming around the truck to stand next to Baron.

Torey nodded and jogged toward them. "Thanks for coming on such short notice. I've got a flight back to Mulberry at six and want to get this all wrapped up. Uncle Paul is already down at the barn."

"Sounds good to us. Let's take a look at this wood, shall we?" Baron said.

Chapter 7

Florian ducked and rolled as Genesis's Bear charged directly at him. He had just enough time to recover and turn to face the Bear once more. "Good charge. This time, I want you to start in human form, charge me as your Bear, and then shift back to human form before you reach me."

"Are you sure? I don't know if I've mastered my shifting like that yet." Genesis looked truly terrified at the idea.

He could understand her hesitation. Genesis had been raised by humans, and the Shifter mentor she claimed to have had did not teach her the proper way. Florian wasn't going to be much help with Bear specific things but general Shifter knowledge and combat skills he could do. The rest she could learn from her crazy grandmother, Betsy.

"Let's just try. If it doesn't work, then we can go back to the meditation I showed you earlier to help you connect with your inner Bear."

Genesis still seemed skeptical, but before Florian could fully prepare himself, she charged. Florian stood his ground. Genesis might not be in full control of her Bear, but Florian had full control of his Falcon. He could shift and be in the air before the Bear got close enough to do damage. He hoped he wouldn't need to shift again as Genesis in her Bear form got closer and closer. He held the Bear's gaze, showing the Bear he wasn't afraid, even as his Falcon pressed against his skin. At the last second before Florian allowed his Falcon to emerge, Genesis shifted back to her human form. Unfortunately, not with enough room to prevent herself from skating straight into Florian's arms.

"See, I knew you could do it. Now, let's try that again, and this time, shift back a second or two before you think you need to," Florian said, taking a step back.

Breathing heavily, Genesis just nodded and trotted back to the other side of the clearing. This time when she charged Florian, she was able to change back in time to stop herself. A smile lit her face, and she started to wiggle her body in a celebratory dance. Florian couldn't help but chuckle, sharing in her joy.

He would never admit it, but he really did enjoy training new Shifters. Florian might have considered it as his job within the Pack, but he'd followed along with his buddies and ended up a Pack enforcer. Good thing Florian also enjoyed a good fight. In a way, it was like teaching, sometimes a Shifter needed a little tough love and a reminder of the rules, and that's where he and the rest of the Pleasure Pack came in. In fact, if he hadn't chosen to be a Pack enforcer, he might never have met Genesis.

Training Genesis certainly wouldn't have happened, which would make getting close to Hunter on his home turf near impossible. The only con of their arrangement was there was no guarantee Hunter would be receptive to his advances, even with the support of Genesis and her mate, Hunter's cousin, Baron.

As it was, they'd already been training for a while, and this had been Florian's first face to face with Hunter on the property. Not that he wasn't basically stalking the man every day. Not just during the day, but also with flying by every night. The urge to be closer to his mate hadn't been this strong since Florian first ended things with Hunter.

"Thank you! Thank you! Thank you! I've made more progress in the few sessions with you than the entire month I spent with my rogue mentor," Genesis said.

She moved to the edge of the clearing where both of their clothes were neatly folded and placed on a fallen log. She took a sip of water from her water bottle before shimmying back into her workout gear.

"Calling it quits already?" Not that Florian really minded. They had done a little hand-to-hand sparring in human form in the open field behind Baron's house for about thirty minutes before moving into the forest to practice combat techniques in Shifter form.

"Yes, as much as I love the progress I've made, I still have human work to do today."

"What do you do for work, anyway? Will it interfere with you living here now?"

Genesis shook her head. "Not at all. Unless the internet goes out, then it might be a problem."

Shifters were known to be a bit cagey about their personal information. Usually that only extended to humans outside of Shifter circles. Then again, Genesis wasn't your average Shifter and had probably lived her life being cagey with everyone. Her hesitance to share her profession was a sign to Florian that while they were beginning to form a good rapport, they weren't friends yet. He didn't pry. Instead, he joined her at the log to take a sip of his own water and pulled on his sweatpants.

"The storms here on the mountain get pretty crazy, but I don't think I need to tell you about that. That being said, I'm sure the Cross family has decent internet."

"Let's hope there aren't too many more storms in the near future. Anyway, thank you for agreeing to train me, even though I know you are really only out here to get back in Hunter's pants." Genesis laughed and headed toward the trail.

Florian followed. "It's not just his pants that I want to get in. I want his heart. He is my mate, and I have to do everything I can to be with him. You, of all people, should understand."

"Yeah, if my Bear hadn't been so obsessed with Baron from the beginning, I don't think I would have even given him a third look."

"Oh, just a second look, huh?" Florian said.

Genesis nudged him in his side.

"Look, these Cross men are fine as hell. There is nothing wrong with taking a second look at such glorious eye candy. I really wasn't expecting all of this. So yeah, I empathize with your plight of having a mate and needing to be with them, but I don't empathize with having my mate and then forcing them away. How was that even possible, Florian? With the story I've been told about my family that should be impossible, right?"

With a heavy sigh, Florian shook his head. "My Falcon gives me so much shit about letting Hunter go but knows I have to be alive for us to have a shot at getting back with him. Every time I shift, he does a fly by on Hunter, regardless of what our mission is. It's been a rough two years and would have been rougher if Hunter wasn't still peripheral in my social circles. Knowing I could see him when I wanted to helped a lot. Even if he couldn't see me. I've been fortunate so far, but my time and grasp on sanity are running out. This is it for me. I won't say I'll keel over and die, but there won't be any coming back from this if my plan to woo Hunter fails."

"Well, he definitely sees you now, and from what I can tell, he likes what he sees."

Genesis pointed toward the cleared field of the Cross Estate, and sure enough, Hunter and Baron were waiting at the other end, Baron's eyes firmly on Genesis and Hunter's on Florian. Florian bit the inside of his cheek to stop the rush of arousal headed straight for his dick. It wouldn't do for him to come waltzing half naked and hard out of the woods with Hunter's cousin's fiancé, as they'd told his family because the Crosses were not humans in the know. In fact, it was better that they didn't know at all that Shifters existed. One of the problems Florian had ignored the first time around. One he couldn't ignore now. There was no telling how Hunter would react to learning there were Shifters out there and Florian was one.

Maybe he wouldn't have to tell Hunter that he was a Shifter. He'd never heard of a Shifter human pairing where the Shifter kept their true identity secret, but that didn't mean it had never happened. The thought was distracting enough that Florian made it all the way across the yard without sporting a dickstand. That didn't mean he wasn't enjoying the pure want on Hunter's face as he took in Florian's bare chest.

"Aren't you cold?" Hunter asked.

"Nah, we worked up quite a sweat on our trail run," Florian said.

"That's no excuse for not wearing a goddamned shirt," Hunter snarled before turning to leave, but Genesis reached out and caught Hunter's arm.

"Uh, Hunter, before you go, I have a huge favor to ask."

Hunter paused for a moment before turning a soft smile on Genesis. "Sure thing, cousin in law. What can I do for you?"

Genesis glanced back at Florian and winked before turning her attention to Hunter. "Florian would probably like to shower before he heads back to Sullah. Do you mind if he borrows yours? I'd let him shower at our place, but um, you know..."

It was obvious Genesis was insinuating she and Baron were going to be occupied and didn't want to delay their coupling. Hunter shook his head before his gaze landed on Florian's body once more. The heat of it trailing up from his navel to his Adam's Apple before meeting his gaze with a hunger all his own. Yeah, Hunter was thinking along the same lines as Genesis, and Florian was all for it. Or rather, should be all for it. He missed Hunter. Missed the way they would tease and play before one of them took over and topped the fuck out of the other. Yeah, those were the days. Then again, these weren't those days, and Florian needed more than just Hunter's body to satisfy his needs. An awkward moment passed as everyone waited for Hunter to speak.

"Sure, he can use my shower, this way." Hunter said before storming off down a well-manicured path deeper into the forest.

Florian followed knowing once they were alone, he would finally get a chance to do the one thing he should have done so much sooner. Apologize.

CHAPTER 8

Hunter tore his gaze away from Florian's sweat glistening abs and marched off toward his cabin. Angry at himself for letting a tantalizing bit of flesh get him to agree to the worst possible idea on the face of the earth. Then again, he'd promised Baron he would quit with the heartbroken act and Genesis had asked him a favor. One she better be prepared to return someday because, fuck. Hunter did not need to have any involvement with Florian Falconer, not now and not ever again.

It had been two fucking years, and Florian had yet to even acknowledge Hunter in public since the incident, let alone apologize, and now, he was here on Hunter's turf. Invading his space and demanding to be acknowledged as if they were long lost buddies or something. Florian agreeing to train Genesis had to be some sort of set up. Baron had basically spelled out as much in the car ride back from the Markham property. Baron had also mentioned Genesis would be going out of town soon, and Hunter would be a total ass for messing up any bonding time Baron had with his fiancé before she left. So yeah, with everything he was feeling right then, he would put it aside and do this one favor. Today only, after that, Florian could take his stank ass back to Sullah in his bright blue Ferrari that had no business being on the gravel drive in front of Baron's cabin.

Hunter's musings kept him sane enough to keep quiet on the short walk to his cabin from Baron's. Yet, he could feel Florian on his heels, hear his deep exhalation as if he too was regretting this decision to shower at Hunter's place. Not that Florian had offered any argument to the contrary. The bastard had just stood there expectantly, looking sexy as hell with his hair pulled back in that long sleek braid. Perfect for pulling while Hunter plowed into his behind.

Hunter immediately stopped that train of thought, but the feel of Florian's hot breath damn near on his neck had him imagining something similar, only this time it was Florian riding him hard. That wouldn't do either, so he slowed his pace until Florian walked alongside him.

"If this is too much, I can just wait until I get home to shower," Florian offered.

"And risk ruining the brand-new leather smell in your Ferrari?" Hunter teased.

Bringing up Florian's prized automobile was a surefire way to distract from the tingling awareness Hunter couldn't ignore whenever Florian was around.

"I wouldn't like it, but it would be my fault alone for not thinking through this arrangement with Genesis," Florian replied.

"Huh, sounds like you entered into an agreement without thinking through the repercussions," Hunter snorted before stomping up the wooden stairs to his porch.

Hunter was pissed all over again, but he welcomed the familiarity and the distance his rage brought him as he let Florian into his home. Hunter kicked his boots off at the door, and if Florian wasn't barefoot, he would have asked him to do the same. Instead, he nodded down the hallway to their right.

"Bathroom is the second door on the right. Towels are in the cabinet over the toilet, and feel free to help yourself to the toiletries," Hunter grumbled.

Florian sighed heavily before reaching out and taking Hunter's hand.

"Hunter, I'm serious. If this is too much..."

Hunter snatched his hand away. "Don't fucking touch me."

Florian let his hand fall to his side. "I'm sorry. I shouldn't have. Fuck! I knew this was going to be hard, but I want to apologize. Not just for today, but for everything. I apologize for not making my intentions clear. I apologize for blurring the lines of our agreement and causing this rift between us. I'm sorry for not apologizing sooner."

"I don't need your apology," Hunter cut him off before he said something to make Hunter want to accept his apology, or worse—let go of the anger he was desperately clinging to for the survival of his heart if nothing else. "I just need you to leave me the fuck alone. You've been perfect at it for the last two years. Why make this harder on both of us?"

"Because this shouldn't have to be hard. It's been two fucking years, and it's just as hard today as it was two years ago. Looking at your face, seeing the anger and the hurt, and knowing it's all my fault. Knowing if I hadn't been such a fucking coward that..." Florian paused and closed his eyes.

The pained expression on his face, the way his fist clenched at his sides, Florian looked to be in absolute physical pain. Hunter couldn't stand it. As much as he tried to deny the connection that had grown with Florian, as much as he wished it had faded in the last two years, Hunter still fucking cared. He crossed the distance between them and pulled Florian into a kiss. Florian's lips were stiff and firm beneath his for a moment before they softened and parted.

His tongue darted out tentatively, and Hunter opened for him. Meeting him tongue for tongue as for a few precious moments nothing mattered but the heat and the overwhelming need to seek comfort in his touch. Comfort from the raging emotions, the black cloud that hung so heavily over both their heads. It wasn't forgiveness that shoved Florian's pants to the ground. It wasn't forgiveness that had Hunter sinking to his knees to capture Florian's growing length between his lips. It was a raw need. So raw, it felt like a million fire ants nipping along his extremities. A burning itch that would only and could only be soothed by skin on skin.

"Ah fuck, Hunt!" Florian groaned, his hips moving back and forth, his rigid staff sliding in and out of Hunter's mouth, building up a new source of heat and sweet agony as Hunter's own erection strained to be set free. Hunter swallowed hard before relaxing his throat to take Florian deeper, gripping his hips to hold them in place while he deep-throated his cock. His gag reflex massaged Florian's length while Hunter fondled Florian's balls, rolling them around with his fingers, squeezing and cupping them before sliding his hands up along Florian's inner thighs and teasing the puckered flesh of his asshole. Florian jerked, and his legs trembled, a harsh cry escaping his lips as his dick pulsed and released down Hunter's throat.

Hunter rocked back onto his heels, letting Florian slide from his mouth. His eyes were watering, and he felt the trail of ejaculate sliding slowly down the back of his throat. "Shower and get out," he breathed before pushing himself onto his feet and marching out the front door.

That was not the fucking plan! We cannot have a thing for Florian anymore.

The way Hunter's erection continued to chafe under the constraints of his denim jeans was evidence to the contrary, but Hunter was a firm believer in mind over matter. Unfortunately, his mind was still replaying what had just happened with Florian. The rawness of his throat, the scent of their sex that had permeated Hunter's living room and now clung to his clothing. All a reminder of just how good things had been between him and Florian before that day. Before Hunter had all but asked outright for Florian to make their no strings fling into a full strings relationship.

As soon as he was out of eyesight from his cabin, he took off running into the tree line, far enough in to be hidden from any prying eyes. He made quick work of undoing his pants so he could free his erection from the confines of the jeans he'd once thought of as roomy for a man of his size. Not even the introduction of the winter chilled air lessened the painful fullness he felt. He grabbed his traitorous dick with a painfully tight grip before hunching over to stroke himself to oblivion with thoughts of Florian's tight ass, naked in his shower, cleaning up the sweat and saliva Hunter had left behind. He screamed in a mix of frustration and ecstasy as he released on a nearby tree stump.

"Damn it all to fucking hell," he growled before shoving himself back into his pants.

Florian is a jerk. An asshole. He nearly ruined your ability to have fun!

Not that Hunter had been having much fun lately. After their break up, if you could call it that, he'd been bitter and angry. He'd concocted a stupid revenge plan involving Florian's sister, and when that fell through, Hunter hadn't been able to move on like nothing had happened.

Had he been a complete saint? Hell no, but man, if things hadn't been less exciting this time around. No matter the flavor, male, female, or any part of the rainbow in between. Hunter may have fucked plenty of people since Florian but none could compare. He could get his rocks off, but his jollies were sorely underrepresented when it didn't involve Florian. That suck and duck session was all the confirmation he needed in that regard. He was out here in the freezing wilderness jacking off like he hadn't done since he was a hormonal ass teenager, and it was all Florian's fault.

Florian, who'd barged back into his life and demanded a place with his actions while once again denying them with his words. Sorry? He was sorry? He should be, but his apology was more than a day late and a dollar short. It was an insult. An insult to what they had and what could have been. The chill finally began to seep in as Hunter's arousal diminished, and his anger, once burning bright, returned to the bitter blue he'd come accustomed to.

Fool me once, shame on you. Fool me twice?

If Florian wanted to fuck, Hunter couldn't say he would be against a rejoining of their flesh but not without having the ground rules out in the open. Hunter was so caught up in his thought he nearly stepped in one of his own bear traps on his way back. Another reminder he had better shit to worry about than Florian Fucking Falconer.

Hunter carefully relocated the trap a little farther from the main trail. The last thing he wanted was to have his family get caught in one because he'd done a poor job of placing them. He had just finished disguising the trap when he heard footsteps approaching.

Florian stood dumbfounded as he watched Hunter's retreat. If his legs weren't so weak from the orgasm Hunter had just sucked from him, he would have followed him immediately. Instead, he sank to the couch, the high of his release not so fulfilling when his Falcon was currently losing their shit.

Go to him!

He doesn't want us.

He does!

Not like how we need him to.

We need our mate!

Trust me. I know.

If you knew, then why hide our mark?

That's complicated.

It's stupid. Go to him now before I do it myself.

Florian felt the Falcon pressing at his skin. The burning itch as feathers sprouted from his pores. Florian was tempted to let the Falcon takeover. Give his human mind a chance to put its full power on solving this problem he'd created for himself. Sure, he'd planned for things to make it to this point sooner rather than later, but this had been too soon. Less than ten minutes alone with Hunter and they'd both fallen right back into their physical attraction to each other. If Florian was going to have any chance at getting Hunter to want him around for good, he needed to work on building a real connection with him.

That being said, Florian was woefully out of depth with making friends with humans. His best friends were all Supernatural. Any human interaction he had was purely business or sex related. The few humans he knew more closely were all mutual acquaintances of his sister Vega. She was the only Shifter he knew that actually preferred to keep human company. Well, at least until recently. Genesis was raised by humans. She also was receptive to helping him with Hunter, as proven by the whole scheme to get him access to the Cross estate.

Maybe the next sparring match he'd throw in a few questions, like hey, what do humans like to do on dates?

Pathetic.

His Falcon's intrusion into his thoughts brought Florian back to the present moment. They were already soaring in the air, his Falcon laser focused on Hunter as he rested against a tree.

Is he crying? Did I make him cry?

Panic and anger at himself sliced through Florian, making his Falcon falter in its circling. They took a bit of a dive before his Falcon caught wind again, but it was enough to give Florian a closer view of Hunter. He was resting on the tree but he wasn't crying. His hunched back was vibrating manically as his arm moved back and forth with familiar jerky movement.

If Florian had lips at that moment, he would have licked them as he watched Hunter angrily beating his dick.

Shall we join him?

No! We should head back and wait for him at his cabin.

We should join.

Florian wasn't about to let the Falcon take complete control in this. He forced the Falcon to head back to the cabin, but he didn't get far before he heard Hunter cursing. His instinct to protect his mate overrode everything else. He quickly course corrected, but Hunter was already trampling angrily back toward the cabin.

Relief came over him until he saw Hunter disappear back into the brush. He landed, not caring that he was completely naked and the questions that would ultimately bring up. All he cared about was getting eyes on his mate. He found Hunter standing on guard in front of what was an obviously prepared trap.

"What the fuck are you doing? Someone could get hurt by this!" Florian cursed, pulling on the chain and revealing the trap.

He was outraged, even knowing no Shifter would ever wander this close to the Cross property. Not any of the larger animals in this area. But Florian knew there was a young child on the property, and Hunter's cousin's wife was a nature photographer and wouldn't think twice about where she was going if she were hunting the perfect shot. Then there was Genesis, who no doubt used these woods to let her Bear roam.

"Excuse you! This is my fucking land. Where do you get off questioning my right to do whatever the hell I please on it?"

"I'm not! I just... What about your family? Do they know these are out here and so close? What about Genesis? She was just running through here during our training!"

"I'm doing this to protect my family! My cousin just got attacked by a fucking bear. Probably the same bear that killed my father and maimed my cousin Braxton!"

Florian scowled and bent over to carefully disarm the trap.

"I'm sorry that your family has had some bad wildlife experiences, but this is not the answer."

"Why the fuck are you naked? Did you come into the woods naked?"

Hunter's question distracted Florian, and instead of disarming the trap, he accidentally set it off. Florian jumped back in time to miss it clamping down on his arm. The loud clang of the metal coming together made both men jump. The suddenness stopped whatever flow of emotion had been happening between them in an instant.

"Shit, look, it's fucking cold out here. Let's get back to the cabin so you can get cleaned up and on your way." Hunter shrugged out of his shirt and walked over to tie it around Florian's waist. The proximity and heat from Hunter's body so close had Florian's cock going stiff, and he bit the inside of his cheek to keep it from being overly noticeable to Hunter. Now was not the time to get distracted by physical urges.

"Thanks," Florian breathed and turned to head back to the main trail. Hunter didn't immediately follow, and he knew Hunter was probably resetting the trap he had laid.

The fear and anger inside Florian at the thought was enough to get him to the cabin and in the shower without a second look back.

CHAPTER 9

Hunter didn't know what to think about what had just happened. Florian showing up in the woods was the last thing he thought would occur, let alone that Florian would be naked and caught him with the bear trap. What was that anyway? Why had Florian followed him into the woods? How had Hunter not noticed Florian following him? Had Florian watched him masturbate, and why hadn't he made his presence known sooner?

All these questions ran through Hunter's head as he followed Florian back to his cabin. Hunter was grateful for all the questions he had, otherwise, he wouldn't have been able to resist watching and hoping a gust of wind would lift this shirt up and reveal Florian's taut backside. If it weren't for Hunter giving Florian his shirt, he may have made a detour to the main house to avoid being in the cabin with Florian, especially as the water in the shower started. It was an insane torture to know the man he wanted so desperately was naked just a few feet away.

With a new shirt and a new resolve, Hunter exited his bedroom. Sure, he should probably wait until Florian was done and possibly initiate a conversation that could answer some of the questions he had. Yet, Hunter didn't feel very brave in that moment. There were too many emotions running through him. So, he did what he always did when he didn't want to face his feelings. He shoved his feet into his boots, grabbed his keys, and went back out to his truck. He drove down the mountain and into Edgewood.

Hunter's preferred way of blowing off some steam would be to visit the Wolf's Den. There were plenty of willing partners to distract Hunter with physical pleasures. Unfortunately, since Florian, those pleasures weren't quite as sweet. The private rooms were also filled with bittersweet memories.

Hunter also didn't feel like making the long drive into Sowell for the second time that day. So instead, he went to his old stomping grounds. The local dive bar in Edgewood was nothing like the Wolf's Den. It being the middle of the day on a weekday, one would think the bar to be closed. The Watershed, however, was open almost twenty-four hours a day to accommodate not just the local folk, but the truckers that came and went hauling Cross Lumber to destinations around the country.

Pushing his way inside the dark, musty bar, the few other patrons paid Hunter no mind as they stared with hollow eyes into their beers and glasses of dark liquor. The old barkeep Jeff was about ninety years old, moved slower than molasses, and couldn't mix a drink to save his life, but he poured heavy and was bursting with outlandish tales to suit your fancy if you were one of the few people who managed to get on his good side. Being a Cross might get Hunter deferential treatment anywhere but here. It was the perfect place for him to sit and wallow without being disturbed.

At least, any other time that would be the case. Unfortunately, as soon as he sat at the bar, Mitchell Jones moved from his perch on the other end and came to sit right next to Hunter. Hunter wouldn't call Mitchell a friend by any stretch of the imagination. The only connection they'd had to one another aside from attending the same schools like literally everyone else in town was Mitchell's cousin being Baron's ex-wife. The Jones family had been really silent about everything that had gone on since the couple's initial separation, but Hunter had a feeling Mitchell had something to say about the matter. Otherwise, he wouldn't have bothered Hunter.

"It's been a while," Mitchell said, clapping Hunter on the back.

"It's been never. Get whatever you need to say off your chest and get moving."

There was no reason for Hunter to play nice, even if he had felt like doing so.

"I heard there's been a lot of new changes up there with you Crosses. A few new people hanging around."

Hunter shook his head and scowled at the man.

"Listen, what my family is up to is none of your business. Never was and never will be. Now, if you don't mind."

Mitchell straightened, a sneer spreading his dry, cracked lips, revealing the years of damage smoking and chewing tobacco had done to his mouth. Hunter leaned away from the man in revulsion, but Mitchell took it as a sign of fear, leaning into the space between them.

"Tell Baron he needs to watch his back. Bringing some darkie whore around here like my cousin meant nothing."

And there it was, the racism wasn't unexpected from someone like Mitchell, and normally, Hunter would call him out on it and move on, but today? No. Today, he was itching to find an outlet for his emotional upheaval and Mitchell had just supplied it. So, he took a calm sip of the beer Jeff had dropped in front of him before cracking his knuckles and punching the guy right in the face. When Mitchell returned the punch with one to Hunter's gut, Hunter smiled.

Perfect.

V: Are you still in Edgewood?

Florian had just climbed into his car, finally realizing Hunter had no intention of returning to the cabin while he was still there. He'd pulled his phone out to check for important messages involving Pack matters, only to find not only a text from his parents saying they were back in town, but also the extremely suspect text from his little sister.

F: Yeah, why?

V: Hunter's been arrested.

Florian began to text her with something along the lines of "what fucking for?" "How do you know?" or "Why should I care?" but Florian cared. He cared a whole helluva lot that Hunter had finally somewhat opened up to him and now he was sitting in some cell. So instead, he called her.

"Vega, tell me everything."

"He said he's at the sheriff's office in Edgewood. He called me because he didn't want his family getting involved. Florian, what the hell happened?" she replied.

"Hell, if I know. Does he need bail? I thought you two weren't close. Why is he calling you with this shit?"

"Hey, don't get jealous. Hunter and I are just friends. Have always been just friends. Besides, that isn't the point. Just go rescue your mate from the clink. It might give you some brownie points toward forgiveness or something."

Florian scowled, even though his sister couldn't see it.

"I'll call you later," Florian hung up and started his car. Not caring a single bit about his paint job and undercarriage as he sped down the gravel drive and out of the Cross Logging compound. From there, it was a mere minute or two to the sheriff's station, even without speeding like a madman, which he did. He drifted to a stop in front of the sheriff's office and was out of the car before he was even certain it was completely in park.

"How may I help you?" an older woman at the front desk asked. She had barely looked up from her women's magazine and was loudly popping a wad of pink bubble gum.

Florian took a deep breath to calm himself before he talked to the woman. He was already on edge, and it wasn't her fault he was here. It wasn't her fault Hunter had done something stupid and ended up arrested. So, he dug up some charm to the best of his current abilities.

"I'm here to bail out Hunter Cross."

The woman looked up then, her eyes going wide before her lids sunk low in what he guessed was her approximation of a sultry look.

"You sure that's who you're looking for, sugar? You a lawyer or something?"

Florian cleared his throat and leaned away from the woman. "No, I am not a lawyer. I am here to bail out my boyfriend, Hunter Cross."

Boyfriend was a big stretch on his part, but it was the quickest way to end whatever shenanigans ran through the woman's head and get her focused on the task at hand. If a lawyer were truly needed, he could reach out to one or maybe call on Ambrose for another favor. He wasn't close enough with anyone in the Cross family to give them a call, and even if he was, Hunter had clearly wished to keep them out of whatever had landed him in jail. The woman smacked her lips and pointed at the clipboard on the counter.

"Sign yourself in, and I'll get someone out here to help you."

Florian signed his name on the paper, and the woman signaled for him to take a seat. Reluctantly, Florian flopped down into a worn-out green vinyl chair in the waiting area. He hoped this wouldn't take too long. It didn't seem like the type of place that would have a backlog of cases or any such thing. Still, ten minutes passed before anyone else came into the space, and when they did, it wasn't anyone to help Florian. In fact, it was someone who would never in a million years be useful to anyone but herself. Christine Cross, or rather, Christine Jones, now that her divorce with Baron was final, strode into the lobby of the sheriff's station with a bad weave, a Gucci knock-off outfit, and a bad attitude.

"Juniper, save me the sass today and just bring my idiot cousin out. Tell Sheriff Moore we drop all charges 'cause I'm sure it was Mitchell's fault."

The lady behind the desk, Juniper, looked up from her magazine again and rolled her eyes.

"Y'all Joneses never know when to quit. I actually rooted for you and Baron to make a real go of it, but you and your greed got the better of you. So no, you will sit and wait like everybody else," Juniper spat.

"Everyone? Really? Not a single person is here but me!" Christine said waving her hand around, but when her head turned and she noticed Florian, her whole demeanor changed.

"Well, well, well, if it isn't one of the infamous Pleasure Pack. What brings you to this side of the mountain?"

Florian groaned internally. The last thing he wanted to do was have any kind of chat with this woman. Juniper's assessment of her was correct down to a T, and Florian had no intention of being caught up in whatever drama she was involved in. Thankfully, Juniper deemed it necessary to finally do her job, and, in the process, save Florian from suffering more than just the curious and calculating stare of Christine Jones.

A minute later, Hunter was walked out of the back in handcuffs. He grinned from ear to ear, despite the bruising and swelling of his face.

"You got lucky the charges were dropped, kid. Don't make this a habit," the officer said to Hunter.

Florian waited for the officer to release Hunter's hands from the cuffs before he pulled him into a hug.

"I hope it was worth it," Florian said, pulling away after Hunter hadn't returned his affection. Not that Florian thought he would, especially with how they had last spoken to each other.

"What are you doing here, Florian?"

"We still have things to discuss. Things best said when not angry and in private, so let's go. I'll take you home."

Hunter looked ready to protest, but one look at Christine and Juniper eyeballing the both of them and Hunter shrugged before storming out of the building. Florian nodded at Juniper before following Hunter out. Except, Hunter wasn't waiting by his car, instead he had bypassed it and headed down the street. Florian caught up and grabbed Hunter's hand.

"Please, Hunt. Just let me take you home. Give me that much time, and if you still want no parts of me, then I'll give you some space."

"Space? Just space?"

Florian sighed. "If I could give you more than that I would, but that's part of the discussion we need to have. Please let me drive you. Even if you managed to get to your car, you still wouldn't be able to see out your swollen eye to make it home safe."

For a moment it looked like Hunter would insist anyway, but then his shoulders slumped and a defeated expression overtook his face.

"Fine, you have as long as it takes to get me home, and that's it. There won't be any second chances at this."

Florian resisted the urge to jump for joy as he led Hunter back to his car.

Hunter slid into the passenger seat of Florian's Ferrari. It was the last place he wanted to be, but the other option was taking a risk with ending up in a hospital instead of home in his bed.

Fuck, I hope no one sees me before I can get home and get cleaned up. The last thing I need is to have Aunt Melinda freaking out that one of her boys has been hurt, again.

As good as it felt to pummel that jackass Mitchell, the ache in his right cheek did nothing to quell the pain in his chest. It was Hunter's first time in Florian's car, and he couldn't even enjoy it.

Florian pulled away from the curb and headed in the direction of the Cross Family Estate.

This wasn't some fun little joyride, and Florian wouldn't be reaching across the console to grab Hunter's hand or thigh. Hunter, for sure, wasn't reaching over to do the same or more. Florian wasn't whisking him away for a night on the town either. All things Hunter had once thought possible, but now only made him that much more uncomfortable on the short ride back to his family's estate.

"You wanted to talk, so talk," Hunter said, breaking the tense silence between them.

"What happened earlier," Florian paused as if considering how best to say what he was going to say next, "I miss you, Hunter. I miss being with you. Not just physically."

Hunter rolled his eyes. "How can you miss me more than physically if that's all we ever had?"

Florian sighed heavily, "Please don't deny that what we had was more than sex."

"I think you have your memories mixed up. I believe it was you who said what we had was just sex; you chose not to try for more. At least, not with me. How is Harvey by the way?"

"We both know this was never about Harvey. There were just so many reasons why you and I couldn't be. The biggest being my inability to see just how important you were to me."

Hunter couldn't help but laugh, even though laughing stretched and pulled on his swollen cheek.

"Call yourself a coward, apologize for leading me on, but don't pretend I ever meant anything to you."

"Hunter, you are everything to me. I just didn't know it then. And now? I know I have a long battle to prove it to you."

"And how exactly do you plan to do that?"

"Well, first, I just needed a chance to be around you again. So, when Genesis asked for help with physical training with the caveat that it had to be at the Cross Estate, I jumped at the chance. I didn't really have a plan. I had hoped that maybe I could get you alone to talk, and I did. It just didn't go how I thought it would."

"That's for sure," Hunter said.

There was no guarantee talking to Florian would solve anything. Especially considering actions spoke way louder than words. Florian's actions said he wanted access to Hunter's body, not his heart. Hunter wasn't willing to risk his heart with Florian again, So, he was done with this conversation. Hunter let his head rest against the seat and turned to look out the window.

Florian released another heavy sigh. It was clear neither of them was getting what they wanted. The silence between them was as heavy as ever, but Hunter took solace in knowing it would only last for the next three minutes it took for Florian to reach the estate. As soon as they were beyond the limits of public access, Hunter would jump out of the car and send Florian on his way. Then, he would have a talk with his cousin Baron about keeping such a short leash on his new girlfriend.

Baron had some serious trust issues with women after what Christine had put him through, but that didn't make it okay for him to keep her cloistered on the estate indefinitely. He needed to loosen the reins a bit. Not just for the sake of Hunter not seeing Florian around in his safe space, but because Hunter truly believed trust and honesty were key to a good stable relationship. Two things he could admit he'd never had with Florian, and at this point, he was sure he never would.

Beep. Beep. Beep. Florian's phone began to ring, breaking the silence. The notification on his dashboard showed it was Vega calling. Florian answered the call, "Yes, I have Hunter with me right now."

"Hey Hunter! I know you're probably pissed that I sent Florian to get you, but he was already on that side of the mountain."

Hunter was pissed it had been Florian who showed up at the jail, but he was also glad not to have had to sit in that tiny musty cell for longer.

"No worries, Vega. I'll be home with Florian out of my hair in no time."

Vega's raucous laughter filled the car. "Florian, I take it that your apology didn't go as planned?"

"Not exactly. Were you calling just to check in about Hunter or was there something else you needed?"

Vega's jovial tone dropped away as she replied to her brother's question, "Yeah, so I stalled as much as possible, but Mom and Dad are growing more and more impatient waiting for you to return."

"Did you tell them I was away on business?"

"Yes, but what business could you possibly be attending to when the rest of the Pleasure Pack is here in Sullah?"

"Fine. I'll be there as fast as I can get there." Florian's grip tightened on the steering wheel before he ended the call.

Hunter's curiosity about Florian's parents was abated by the reminder that Florian was still hiding, and not just from Hunter.

"I guess you better hurry and drop me off," Hunter said.

Florian's chiseled jaw twitched before a mask of indifference slid back into place. It seemed his penchant for controlling things extended deeper than Hunter had imagined. As the turn off approached for the Cross Estate, Florian kept going.

"Florian. What are you doing?" Hunter kept his tone level. He wanted to scream, but he could see the tension in Florian's frame, from his ramrod straight back to the slight press of his fingertips into the leather on the steering wheel. Raising his voice would do nothing but make Florian's driving more reckless, and the two-lane road through the pass was not the place for an argument.

"I promise I'm not kidnapping you. At least, not really. I just need to handle this stuff back home as soon as possible, and I figure if you're trying to keep your arrest and your bar fight away from your family, that maybe a little weekend trip might be your best option."

"So, you're just making decisions for me now?"

"Sorry? I know it's not ideal, but maybe this can be beneficial for both of us. You will get to see another side of me, perhaps one you like better than the Florian you first met and came to hate."

In everything the man just said, the only thing Hunter actually heard was Florian thought Hunter hated him. That couldn't be further from the truth. Hunter didn't hate Florian. He hated what Florian did to them, to him.

"I don't hate you, Florian, but I do hate whatever this is."

"I'm sorry."

"No, you're not."

"Hunter, it's your choice. You will always have a choice. I can turn around."

"Sure, Florian, like any of this was my choice." Hunter snorted; the way Florian was driving they were halfway through the pass already. No place to safely turn around until they reached the other side. Would Florian really turn around when he was only minutes from Sullah? Hunter didn't think so.

The car slowed as Florian looked toward Hunter, but the moment for Florian to make this whole ordeal any less of a shit show was over.

"Handle your business, Florian, but you really need to reevaluate your idea of what choice is," Hunter grumbled.

CHAPTER 10

Hunter didn't even pretend like he wasn't going to explore the fuck out of Florian's home. As much as he wanted to deny it, Hunter was intrigued to get a glimpse of what the real Florian was like. He could put up all the pretenses he wanted in the outer world, but everyone knew a man's home told all you needed to know about them. Was Florian as put together as he liked to portray to the outside world? Hunter was going to find out. So far, the living room hadn't been much of a shock. A collage of neutral colors, some custom wood built-ins Hunter had to admit were nice, even if his cousin Braxton would have done a much nicer job, and stone work mixed with a touch of modern finishes to the open kitchen. The neutral brown leather couch sat positioned in front of a stone fireplace and a fifty-inch television Florian probably watched his favorite soccer team on, because Florian was definitely the type of guy to go all in for the World Cup but scoff at the barbarism of America's favorite pastime.

On the live edge mantle, just below the TV, was a line of photographs. Hunter studied them closer and couldn't help the smile that curved his lips up so high his cheeks hurt. The first photo showed Florian and the rest of the Pleasure Pack in their teens. Hunter recognized Calix, Florian, Aletris, and Jacinto, but there was a smaller Asian boy in the photo he couldn't place. He stood at the edge of the group, just barely in the shot. It almost seemed as if the kid had photo bombed the group, if it hadn't been for Florian's hand on the kid's shoulder.

A twinge of jealousy pricked Hunter before he turned his gaze to the next photo. This one was of Florian and Vega posing in front of the Sowell Gate High Prom background. Hunter had a similar photo somewhere back home. He'd crashed the prom with his high school buddies and managed to get a quick photo in before going through with their drunken prom night pranking.

Florian looked hot as fuck, even back then. His black suit, while not as fashionable as what he'd wear today, had been perfectly tailored to his tall muscular frame. His long black hair left loose, flowing over his shoulders in long silken strands. Yeah, if Hunter had been a little bit braver when it came to his preferences, he may have made his move on Florian back then. Then again, even if he'd known Florian's preference for men in those days, there had also been plenty of other reasons for the two of them to never think about it. Instead of tracks, since there were no train tracks in the Sowell Gate area, they were a wrong side of the mountain tale. A pair of star-crossed lovers, where only Hunter had died in the court of public opinion.

Hunter tried to cling to the tiny spark of anger that had resurfaced, but it faded just as quickly as his gaze traveled to Vega in the photo. She looked less than pleased to have been escorted to prom by her brother. Vega's dress was much less flattering. The pink, sparkly sheath had a high neckline and a long train. More reminiscent of a mother-of-the–bride dress, if the bride really hated their mother. The next photo on the mantel was of what Hunter assumed was the entire Falconer clan. About ten people were gathered together, almost none of them looking toward the camera or even smiling. The adults looked either grim or stoic as they stood before the stunning backdrop of the Sowell Gate Mountains.

Florian and Vega stood next to two other teens, looking stiff and miserable while a gaggle of young, mostly naked children rough-housed at their feet. Not usually the kind of photo one would display proudly on a mantle, but it only reminded Hunter that there were layers to Florian Falconer he had yet to uncover. Florian obviously valued family, but outside of the photos with Vega and his best friends, it was clear all wasn't as rosy as Florian liked to portray.

Hunter could understand that as the Crosses were far from the perfect family themselves. As much as Hunter missed his father, he knew his father would never have been okay with his only son being with another man. As far as Hunter's mother? Between all the rumors and conflicting stories he'd been told about his parent's relationship and the circumstances of the accident that killed her, Hunter didn't know much about her either.

He moved away from the mantle and the intrusive thoughts about his own family dynamics. Choosing instead to explore the place fur-ther. The first door he encountered just before entering the hallway turned out to be a small powder room, nothing interesting to see there. He went down the hall, opening more doors that revealed an equally bland office space and a room that must have once belonged to Vega. Her perfume still lingered in the space, and Hunter smiled to himself. He'd known Florian and Vega were close, but he never expected them to have lived together as adults.

Then the hall split, each side ending with a single door. On one end, the hall was lined with close-up photographs of different flowers and landscape designs. Not at all anything Florian would be interested in, and while Hunter was curious about what was held behind that door, he found it was locked and could only be opened with a key. Hunter could have picked the lock, but he wasn't sure how much time he would have before Florian returned, and as much as he would love to see what Florian kept under lock and key, he didn't want to get caught snooping too much.

So, he turned around and headed the other direction. The other hallway was bare and the door unlocked. He opened it, and the smell of Florian's favorite cologne engulfed him. Wrapping around him like a warm cozy blanket and beckoning him inside. He accepted the invitation, eyeing the large king-sized bed with its neatly spread gray comforter and exactly two pillows in matching gray propped against the horizontal wood planks of the floor to ceiling headboard.

An image of him and Florian making a mess of his perfectly tucked and smoothed sheets came to mind. He took a step closer, running his hand along the smooth fabric. He gripped it in his hand and pulled, dragging the bedding to the floor before marching to the head of the bed and tossing the pillows to the floor.

Yeah, that was much better. Florian needed a little chaos in his life, and Hunter was just the man for the job, at least for this weekend. Hunter had made up his mind in the car. He would have his fun with Florian, get him out of his system once and for all. Leaving Florian to deal with the fallout this time.

Hunter moved away from the bed and walked to Florian's closet. Once again, there seemed to be no surprises there. He walked further into the space and stopped as he saw a familiar outfit hanging as if on display at the back of the closet. His body jolted in shock before a warmth spread through him and a smile tugged at his lips. It was the outfit Florian had worn the night they'd admitted their attraction for one another. Hunter was intrigued by the fact he'd kept it at all, let alone that it was displayed so prominently in his personal space. He would just ignore the symbolism of it being on full display but still tucked away in the closet. The one room with a little color and flare.

Hunter had stepped out of the closet a long time ago and had no intention of ever going back. Hunter grabbed the hanger holding his old clothes and carried them out of the closet. He needed a change of clothes and, he paused to sniff himself, a good shower to rinse away the stench of alcohol and small town lock up.

Florian glanced back at his house while his friends continued to make jokes about his predicament.

"Have you even told him you're a Shifter yet?"

Calix's question brought Florian's attention back to his friends. His face fell as he thought of the biggest hurdle he had yet to jump with Hunter. If what happened at Hunter's place was any indication, Hunter was open to continuing the physical aspect of their relationship. This weekend, Florian had planned to rekindle the emotional one. He figured once he had Hunter thoroughly hooked again, sharing the secret of his shifting abilities would be easier. He just needed Hunter invested in them as a couple first.

"I can tell by the constipated look on your face that you haven't," Yarrow said, shaking his head disapprovingly.

"It's not that simple. I'm already up against so much with Hunter right now," Florian replied.

Jacinto patted Florian's back. "Just do it. Like ripping off a band-aid."

Calix shook his head. "You've already broken his trust and his heart once. It's better to start with honesty."

Aletris laughed, "Wow, when Calix starts giving good relationship advice, you know the universe is really rooting for this relationship to work."

Yarrow continued to study Florian, making him squirm under the Alpha's scrutiny before he spoke again.

"Tell Hunter the truth tonight. Trust in the fates, and trust in your mate."

Florian's shoulders relaxed as he realized this was his friends' round-about version of a pep talk. They were right. Hunter deserved the truth. Especially after everything that had happened between them. How could he expect Hunter to trust him when it was obvious he was hiding such a huge part of who he was? He wanted Hunter to love all of him. Not just the carefully crafted image he portrayed.

"Alright, but I need to talk to my parents first. I don't want them barging in and making a mess of things before I get a chance to explain to Hunter." Florian pulled out his phone and texted Vega that he would meet her at their parent's cabin up the mountain.

He didn't want to leave Hunter alone too long, but he needed to handle this first.

"Go handle your business. I can crash with this asshole for the weekend," Jacinto said, and nodded toward Aletris.

Aletris rolled his eyes but nodded in the affirmative. Florian smirked and tucked his phone away.

"If all things go as planned, you might need a new residence soon."

Jacinto shook his head. "Fates willing."

Florian laughed before turning toward the nearby tree line. He shrugged out of his joggers and shifted into his Falcon. It would be quicker to reach his family cabin by air. Taking flight, he had to force his Falcon to fly away from the cabin and away from Hunter. His Falcon was becoming more impatient with Florian when it came to claiming their mate. He allowed one pass over of the cabin before taking back control and heading to his parent's place. He landed in front of the porch and shifted back to human form just as the front door opened. Vega scowled at Florian before tossing him a pair of sweatpants and a t-shirt.

"Hurry up, so we can get this over with," she grumbled.

Florian sighed. As much as he and Vega loved their parents, as soon as they had reached mating age, it seemed all their parents cared about was getting them both mated and popping out baby Falcons. It had turned their once adoration into a grudging tolerance of their antics.

Case in point, the tense atmosphere as Florian walked into the house and realized his parents had returned from their trip with company. A man and a woman sat side by side on the family's couch, sipping tea, while his mother rambled on about how capable a Shifter mate he and Vega would be. She barely stopped in her praises to look up and acknowledge that Florian had arrived.

At least their father wasn't as blinded in their matchmaking scheme. He stood and gave Florian a big hug.

"Glad you could finally join us," his father said gruffly before gesturing for Florian to come into the room.

"Florian, this is Karen and Kareem from the Mulberry Pack. You remember we took that cruise one summer, and you guys just hit it off so well? We've kept in touch with their parents."

Florian put a hand up to stop his mother, knowing full well that despite connecting with the pair as kids, he and Vega had zero interest in reconnecting with them now. Even just the reminder of that awful cruise made his stomach turn.

"I'm sorry if my parents and yours mislead you about my availability, but I have already met my fated mate."

There was no point in sugar coating it or letting these people down easy. He didn't have the time or the patience for it. Florian's mother gasped and pressed a hand to her cheek.

"Since when? Why is this the first I've heard about this?"

Vega smirked. "Mother, I tried to tell you when you called last week."

Their mother turned to Vega as if she had just slapped her. "You didn't mention a single thing about Florian, except that he was passed over for the position as Beta of the Pack."

Florian fought the urge to roll his eyes. He had no intention of ever being Pack Beta. Sure, he enjoyed being a Pack enforcer, but being the Pack Beta would take too much of his time. He turned to the two now uncomfortable newcomers on his parent's couch.

"Again, I apologize for my parents misleading you. I hope you enjoy your stay here in Sowell City, but I must get back to my mate," he said curtly.

Florian turned on his heel and started to march right back out the door. He'd never been this outright rude, but he was so close to making Hunter his for good. The last thing he wanted would be to jeopardize things with him again.

Florian had just stripped off the shirt Vega had given him in preparation for his shift when his father came up behind him.

"Hold on a minute, son," he said.

Florian stilled and bit back a heavy sigh. "Yes, Dad?"

"You know your mother and I just want to see you happy. We'd love to meet your mate. Tonight, at dinner?"

Florian ran his hand over his face. He wasn't sure he could convince Hunter into dinner with his parents. Hell, he'd basically kidnapped Hunter to get him to his place.

"Not tonight, but soon." He didn't have to look to know his father wore a disappointed look on his face. He could feel it radiating against his back.

Florian shucked off his sweats and carefully folded them before shifting into his Falcon. At top speed, they rushed through the air to get back to their mate. To get back to Hunter, and maybe, just maybe, into his arms. Despite his Falcon protesting, Florian took the time to get properly redressed before entering his home. He expected Hunter to be on the couch watching TV, or maybe reading one of the coffee table books Jacinto insisted on keeping out.

To his surprise, Hunter wasn't in the living room.

"Hunter?" Florian called out, but no answer came. For a split-second, Florian panicked and was about to head back out the door, almost certain Hunter had changed his mind and made a run for it, but before he got two steps, he realized the water was running in the back of the house.

His eyes drifted closed, and he grunted as his dick hardened in his pants. Fuck. Hunter was in the shower. His shower. Just like he'd been naked in Hunter's shower earlier. The scent of Hunter's body wash still clung to his skin, just as Florian was sure his would linger on Hunter's. The thought of Hunter carrying his scent, even if it wasn't his mating scent, was still enough to fan the flames of his need to claim Hunter as his once and for all.

Before he realized it, Florian's body had carried him to his bedroom doorway. He would have been further if the sight in front of him hadn't brought him up short. His bedroom door was open, revealing the mess Hunter had made of his sheets. The sight should have pissed Florian off. He liked things to be neat and orderly, but all he could think about was Hunter naked in his shower, slathering himself with Florian's favorite products after rumpling his sheets. Not just rumpling them but tossing them about, half on the floor, some scrunched up on the edge.

Florian gripped himself. Yeah, he was a fucking statue right now. Rock hard and standing straight up at the scene, which mimicked his heart's desires. To have Hunter in his bed, to have made that mess while rolling around on his mattress. Twisting the sheets around their limbs as they wrestled for who would top who.

His hands steadily stroked his flesh, imagining Hunter's firm calloused fist jerking him off as he positioned himself behind him. The warmth of his chest on his back, the guttural groan when he eased himself between Florian's ass cheeks.

The bathroom door opened, jolting Florian out of his imagination. Guiltily, he dropped his hold on his dick, only to stagger back against the door frame. His imagination had nothing on the sight of Hunter emerging out of a steam cloud, water droplets trailing from his tousled wet locks, down the rippling planes of his abs, and further still to the white towel slung low over his hips.

When Florian finally dragged his gaze back up to Hunter's face, he wore the sexiest smirk.

"Like what you see?"

"You know I do."

"Then come over here and take it."

As tempting as the proposition was, Florian needed to try to keep a level head. They needed to have a serious conversation before Florian had any chance of making Hunter his mate.

"We need to talk," Florian said.

"I don't want to talk."

Hunter sidled closer, letting the towel around his waist slip further down, revealing another tantalizing inch of skin. Sweat broke out across Florian's brow as he played mental tug of war with his Falcon.

The bird screeched inside, pressing at his skin. To be allowed to claim their mate once and for all, but Florian couldn't allow them to force this on Hunter. It needed to be his choice. Florian tore his gaze away from Hunter and focused on the wall behind his left ear.

"I'll wait in the living room while you get dressed." Florian turned to leave the bedroom, but Hunter closed the distance between them, grabbing Florian by the waist.

"Are you running again, Flor? You dragged me back in. For what? To keep playing games? I don't think so," Hunter breathed against his ear.

Florian bit his lip, leaning back into Hunter as his hands slid into his pants and gripped Florian hard, almost to the point of pain.

"You think I'll let you just toy with me again? Let you have your way with me, then kick me right back to the curb?" Hunter stroked him slow and tight. The friction a slow burn, like the tension simmering between them.

Florian grabbed Hunter's hand to still his movements. He needed a moment to regain some modicum of control before he answered. "This isn't a game. It was never a game."

Hunter used his other hand to remove Florian's grip from his before continuing to stroke Florian into a blinding lust. His head spun; his legs quivered as Hunter brought him to the brink of madness. "Oh, this is a game alright, only this time I plan to win. I plan to strip you of all that precious control until you have no option but to show me the truth. Can you do that, Flor? Can you be completely fucking honest for once?"

Releasing a heady breath, Florian fought the urge to give in. To relax into Hunter's embrace and let things play out the way Hunter wanted. He knew it wouldn't serve his purpose to let Hunter have his way like this. Hunter had said it himself. He still thought of this, of them, as a game, and Florian wouldn't allow it. Not this time. However, he would give Hunter one thing he asked for. His truth.

"You want the truth?"

"Always," Hunter said, thrusting his hips forward, rubbing his long shaft against Florian's ass.

If his intent was to throw Florian off balance, it was working. Florian spread his legs wider and leaned forward to brace himself against the door frame. Hunter continued to rock into him. The tip of his penis glancing over Florian's puckered hole, teasing him with what they both so desperately wanted. The physical connection between them was still so strong, despite years of being apart.

"The truth..." Florian wasn't able to finish the sentence as the first waves of impending orgasm stole his concentration, "Hunt, please. I can't..."

"Oh yeah, this is exactly where I want you. Come on, Flor. Your truth." Hunter's grip grew tighter, his movements faster, focusing on the middle of his dick up to the tip and back.

Florian's head dropped forward; his breathing labored. He hunched over, thrusting into Hunter's hands until the chase was all he could think about. He was going to blow his load all over the wall, but at the last second, Hunter pulled away with a hiss.

Florian collapsed against the wall, catching his breath before turning to find Hunter retreating. One hand gripping his own cock, the other gripping his red hair in frustration. He stood naked before Florian, looking sexy as fuck, but what really got Florian's attention was the new addition to Hunter's tattoo.

Right in the center of his chest, directly above his heart, was a Falcon. Wings spread wide, talons reaching out. The coloring was almost identical to Florian's own Falcon. The blazing lust he felt tempered into an all-encompassing ache. Hunter had already marked himself as his, and he didn't even know it.

Mate him.

Moving as if on auto pilot, Florian closed the distance between them and placed his hand directly over the tattoo before leaning down to place a kiss on Hunter's sternum. Hunter groaned and began to stroke himself. His hand fell from his hair to Florian's shoulder before applying enough pressure to force Florian to his knees in front of him. Licking his lips, Florian stared up at Hunter. He knew what Hunter wanted, what he needed, but he wanted to express to Hunter just how much he needed him back. Not just for tonight, but for forever. As if sensing Florian was about to make the mood more serious, Hunter put a finger to his lips.

"If the next words out of your mouth aren't about a scene or who's topping tonight, I don't want to hear it. I came for the sex, Florian, that's all."

Hunter's words were almost enough to make Florian stop. He sat back on his haunches, ready to push to his feet. Ready to pull his pants back up and force Hunter to have the conversation they desperately needed to have. Almost, but the pleading look in Hunter's eyes was his undoing. Talking would have to wait. "No scene tonight. Just you and me. Own me, Hunter."

CHAPTER 11

This was a dream. It had to be. There was no way this could be real. Florian on his knees in front of him, begging Hunter to own him. It was the stuff of fantasy and nightmare all at once. His heart beat so fast it felt as if it would beat right out of Hunter's chest. Forcing a false bravado, Hunter smirked down at Florian.

"You want me to top tonight? Are you sure you can handle that?"

Florian licked his lips and leaned close enough that his warm breath tickled the tip of Hunter's dick. It was all Hunter could do not to shove his cock right between those soft lips and put an end to whatever damning statement was about to come next. "You said you wanted to fuck. I admit I screwed you over in the past. So, it's only fair that you get to screw me back. So, fuck me. Fuck me with all your anger, all your disappointment. Fuck me until all the shit between us is washed away with sweat and cum and outrageous orgasms. Then when we are exhausted, when all the childish behavior that came between us is exorcized, we'll talk like the grown ass men we are."

Hunter took another step back, the hunger in his eyes softening at the reminder of their history together. Florian hated that he was the reason for that sadness, for the dimming of Hunter's light. It clawed at him, at his heart, and all he could think about was making sure he was never the cause of it again. He grabbed Hunter by the waist and pulled him forward. His lips parted, sliding over Hunter's flesh, sending electric heat up his shaft. Hunter moaned, his hand coming up to grip Florian's head, grinding his pelvis into his face as Florian took every inch of his cock in his mouth.

If Hunter had thought he'd given his body enough time and distance to take the edge of the freight train of an orgasm that had threatened to overcome him, he was so incredibly wrong. The searing heat of Florian's tongue on his flesh, the sloppy wet suction of his cheeks, his fingertips burrowing into his hips and ensuring Hunter could only achieve short choppy thrusts that tapped the back of Florian's throat, all brought it roaring back into the station, no breaks.

The tingling electricity spread from his cock through the rest of his body; his thighs clenched, back bowed. A stream of obscenities poured from his mouth as his cum shot down Florian's throat.

"Fuck! Shit! Fuck! Ugh, damn it!" He stumbled back until he fell on the bed, mind completely wiped of all intelligent thought.

Florian appeared by his side, wiping his mouth with the back of his hand. A mischievous glint in his eyes had Hunter grinning from ear to ear. This was what he wanted. Not to talk, not to explore the emotions swirling inside, but to fuck. To feel Florian's hands and mouth all over his body. To push them both to their physical limits of pleasure. The look in Florian's eyes promised all of that and more.

Beep. Beep. Beeep.

Both men stilled at the interruption of Florian's phone. The real world intruding on their time together.

"Let it ring," Hunter said, reaching for Florian, who sank eagerly into his open arms.

Florian leaned in for the kiss. *Beep. Beep. Beeep.*

Hunter held the back of Florian's head, urging him with the press of his lips to ignore it. Florian smiled against his mouth before pulling away.

"Let me just make sure it's not an emergency," Florian said, climbing off the bed.

Hunter rubbed his hand over his face to hide the disappointment he felt. "Sure, why not?"

Florian grabbed his clothes from the floor and retrieved his phone from his pocket before depositing the clothes in the hamper by the door. Watching Florian bend over in front of him, waving his thick muscular cheeks in Hunter's face achieved the same reactions as a matador's red cape to a bull. Hunter gripped the sheets to keep from charging. To keep himself firmly on Florian's exquisite mattress and not launching forward to continue what had been so rudely interrupted.

Instead, Hunter took a minute to admire Florian's naked body while he tapped out a text to whoever had called. The way his golden skin glistened with a light sheen of sweat, highlighting the deep crevices that outlined his washboard abs. The perfect V-shaped edges that tapered down from his hips, drawing the eye to his glorious cock. Hunter swallowed to keep from drooling at the sight. Not a single hair impeded Hunter's view of what Florian was packing.

So much for restraint. Hunter pushed off the bed, ready to drag Florian back into it, but Florian put up a hand.

"Let me get cleaned up first, and then we can continue where we left off," Florian said before disappearing into the bathroom.

Hunter started to follow, but Florian closed the door in his face. He gripped and flexed his hands to keep from punching the door in frustration. Maybe he needed to rethink restarting anything with

Florian. The man was infinitely more confusing this time around, going from hot to cold faster than his Ferrari hit 100mph. He knew Florian had issues with relinquishing control, had known his claims of letting Hunter be in charge would be short-lived, but not this short. Once again, Florian was doing as he pleased without a single thought about Hunter's feelings. Only this time, Hunter wasn't about to just let it go.

Florian stood under the freezing cold water that cascaded from his rainfall showerhead. The shock to his overheated body was enough to keep his dick in check for now, but not the racing of his heart, or the twisting nerves in his stomach. Was this really happening? Was he really about to let Hunter take control for the night? Could Florian even do it? Even if he could, even if things went exactly as he hoped, there was still the hurdle of getting Hunter to agree to dinner with his parents. That's what all the texts and calls had been about. Vega and his mother both had implored him to make sure dinner happened soon. The best he could offer them was tomorrow night. It wasn't a lot of time, and he needed every minute.

"I should just cancel the dinner," he muttered to himself.

That would have been the safest decision, but then he risked his parents making a surprise visit to his cabin. He could lock the door and pretend he wasn't home. Maybe bite the bullet and drive Hunter back to the Cross estate? Then what?

As his mate, Hunter would have to meet them, eventually. The Falcon was out of the bag when it came to those closest to him knowing he had found his fated mate. Yet, his family was not a fan of the Crosses.

Hell, most Shifters weren't. He couldn't think of any recent tragic run-ins with his family line. The last being his Great Uncle who'd been shot by one of Hunter's distant cousins. He hadn't died from the encounter, but the family remembered.

Would his parents bring it up at dinner? Probably not. Hopefully not. Then there was the fact Hunter had dated Vega, and the fact his parents were desperate for grandchildren. He wouldn't put it past them to bring up the procreation issue. Florian did want kids one day, but that obviously had never been a topic of conversation with Hunter.

"I'm well and truly fucked," Florian grumbled. He shut off the water and reached for the towel he usually kept neatly folded on the counter just outside the shower.

He frowned when he realized it wasn't there, for a moment forgetting Hunter had just been in his shower less than an hour before. He'd been on autopilot as soon as he'd shut the door in Hunter's face. Florian had known Hunter would only aim to distract him if he'd allowed him to follow. Yet, he'd still been a distraction, and clearly a major disruption to Florian's status quo. As if this situation needed any extra layer of chaos thrown in.

Florian reached for his body oil. He could blow dry his hair and let his body air dry. It wasn't his preferred method, but the extra time and space he had away from Hunter, the more time he had to regain some semblance of control. Not just of the situation, but of himself.

When Florian finally emerged from the bathroom, he half expected Hunter to have bolted. Instead, Hunter lounged on the bed in a pair of Florian's pajama pants.

"I see you've been in my closet," Florian said.

"Well, I couldn't keep walking around in the clothes you bailed me out in," Hunter replied.

"I'm surprised you didn't leave," Florian said, walking into the closet. He kept his gaze on any and everything but Hunter.

Having Hunter in his private space was already enough temptation. Him in Florian's own pajamas was like throwing gasoline on his already blazing arousal. As much as Florian wanted to act on the impulse, he knew talking needed to happen sooner rather than later, and he couldn't allow Hunter to distract him from that any longer.

"I'm not surprised you're already reneging on your promises," Hunter shot back.

A shot of ice traveled through Florian's veins at Hunter's words. He finished pulling his pajama shirt over his head before peeking his head out of the closet. Hunter was still lounging on Florian's torn apart bed. A cocky grin spread across Hunter's face when he saw the panic Florian had forgotten to hide.

Of course, Hunter couldn't resist teasing Florian, even if he'd one hundred percent meant the words he said.

"I keep my promises, Hunter. I have every intention of letting you own me later."

"Later? I might not be here later," Hunter scoffed.

"So, you're planning to run away this time?"

"Not yet. I'm too curious about what the real Florian is like."

"You've always known the real Florian." Florian shook his head and disappeared back into the closet to finish getting dressed.

"I've known what you're like in bed, but not much else."

"What would you like to know?"

"Tell me about your parents?"

"They like to travel more than they liked actually raising the children they brought into the world."

"You sound bitter," Hunter replied.

"Not bitter. I know they love us in their own way. I just don't care for how they show it."

There was a brief moment of silence that lasted just long enough for Florian to come rushing out of the closet to make sure Hunter hadn't left. Hunter was still there, only he was bent over the bed trying to reposition the sheets he'd tossed about earlier.

"Are you trying to fix the bed?"

Hunter paused in what he was doing, a faint bit of red rushing to his cheeks. "Maybe? Do they know?"

Florian frowned. "Do they know what?"

"That you're gay."

"Yes."

"And are they okay with that?"

"Yes, except they want grandkids. My older siblings weren't as forgiving about my parents' absentee status and don't speak to them. My younger siblings, aside from Vega, are too young for that to be a thing yet.

Hunter snorted, "What they want doesn't matter. If you don't want kids, then they can't force you to have them."

"No, they can't, but whether or not I have them in the future is still up in the air," Florian answered honestly. Although, he left out the most important part of his answer. That having kids all depended on if Hunter wanted kids.

"In the air because?"

Hunter tossed the blanket over the wonky half smoothed covers and placed his hands on his hips to admire what Florian assumed Hunter believed was a completed job. Florian moved over to the bed to fix the mess Hunter had created.

"Because I don't know if the man I want to spend my life with wants kids." Florian eyed the bed once more before deciding it would probably be better just to change the sheets, anyway. He tore everything off the bed and deposited it in the hamper.

"Well, when you meet that man, I hope you give them a real choice in the matter instead of just manipulating them," Hunter said.

There was no mistaking the anger in Hunter's tone. The man was going to drive Florian insane much quicker than being without him had.

Hunter didn't understand the anger that coursed through him like acid in his veins. So what if Florian was on the fence about kids? So what if Florian didn't see Hunter as the man he wanted to raise those not yet kids with? No, he wasn't angry about that.

Yes, you are.

He was angry that he'd even tried to fix Florian's bed. Angry that Florian didn't even see him as good enough for that simple task.

Partly true, but don't fool yourself.

The voice in Hunter's head wouldn't let him avoid the truth. Not this time. Really, not ever. The voice, as he liked to call it because it wasn't quite his voice but still part of him, had been the one to urge him to flirt with Florian. The voice had been the one to convince him what they had was more than just awesome sex.

Now in his anger, he put up a mental block against that voice. Listening to it is what led him here in the first place. There was nothing more it could say to convince Hunter to stick around after this weekend. That task was all up to Florian, and he was doing a real shit job of it.

Florian moved around the bed and pulled Hunter to him. "If I wasn't being as clear as I thought, I mean you, Hunter. I see my future with you."

Pretty words, but did he mean them? Did Florian really see them together, want kids with Hunter? Hunter had never really given thought to kids much other than avoiding having them. "I think you need to convince me of forever before we have any conversation about kids."

"And that is what I'm trying to do. Earlier, you asked me to tell you the truth, and I have. Now I'd like to show you if you'll let me," Florian said, groping Hunter's groin.

After the way Florian had sucked him off earlier, Hunter was surprised he was as rock hard as he was. Hunter could deny the intense attraction he had for Florian all he wanted, but when it really came down to it? Hunter was putty for the man.

"Fucking out our feelings still on the table?"

The dark hunger in Florian's eyes would have been answer enough, but Florian pulled Hunter closer. His grip on Hunter's chin was firm but not painful as he smashed his lips against Hunter's. The minty freshness of Florian's toothpaste mingled with the warm sweetness of Florian's mouth, sending Hunter's arousal through the roof.

"Clothes off." Hunter couldn't have told you if it was him or Florian who issued the command. All he knew was he was already kicking the loose pajama pants down his legs. Putting just enough space between him and Florian so he could also lift Florian's shirt back over his head.

There shouldn't have even been so many layers of clothing between them. They'd both known what the end game of the evening was meant to be, and it wasn't talking. At least, not for Hunter. He gripped and kneaded Florian's back before shoving the man down onto the bed he'd so perfectly spread.

"Lube?"

"Drawer. Bedside table." Florian nodded his head to the right side before climbing higher on the bed.

Hunter went to the table, grabbed the bottle of lube, and squeezed a healthy amount into his hand.

"Turn around, ass up," Hunter demanded.

Florian raised an eyebrow at him, "What, no foreplay?"

Hunter stroked his dick, coating it with the thick anal lube. "Not what you asked for."

Florian shrugged before turning onto his stomach and pushing up to his hands and knees. The bed dipped as Hunter knelt on the bed. He poured another generous helping of lube on his hand before rubbing it all over Florian's puckered hole. Foreplay wasn't happening, but Hunter wasn't going to hurt Florian. He teased him, testing the elasticity of Florian's ass with his fingers. In the open table drawer, Hunter had seen a few anal toys that would get Florian prepped for his length and girth, but Hunter was too impatient for that.

Besides, with the way Florian already rocked back and forth along the length of his middle finger, it appeared that wouldn't be entirely necessary. Hunter stretched him further by inserting another lube coated finger, then another. Florian's breathing went ragged and choppy, his hips picking up the pace as Hunter stretched him even further.

Hunter leaned forward until his front was pressed against Florian's back. He suckled on Florian's earlobe until Florian shivered, his muscles relaxing around his fingers. "You ready for me, Flor? You think you can handle my monster cock in your ass?"

"Fuck me, Hunt. Own me," Florian groaned barely above a whisper.

Hunter didn't have to be told twice. He removed his fingers and replaced them with his cock before Florian's sphincter had a chance to fully recover. Both men groaned aloud as Hunter slid right in.

"Fuck!"

Florian rested his chest on the bed and reached back, grabbing Hunter's thighs. Holding him still as his muscles gripped tight around the base of Hunter's cock. Hunter let out a slow breath, welcoming the stillness as Florian's hot ass worked his cock. He didn't linger, however; the stillness became too still. He needed to feel that same tightness running up and down his length. He spread his legs wide, creating a sturdy base, before wrapping Florian's long silky locs around his fist. He pulled Florian up, forcing him back on his hands and knees.

"Safe word is pineapple. Use it if I get too rough or you need a break."

"I think I can handle it, Hunter," Florian said.

"Pineapple, Flor. That's the only saving grace from what I'm about to unleash on you." Hunter didn't give Florian a chance to respond. He slid out a few inches before slamming his hips forward. Then again, and again, until all Hunter could feel was the slide of Florian's flesh against his.

Thighs clenched and released as he thrust his pelvis forward and back, sweat dripping down his face, down his abs. Florian's ass slammed back to meet him. His guttural moans drove Hunter closer to his breaking point.

They'd been going at it for who knows how long. Hunter may not have been willing to admit it out loud, but Florian had been right about Hunter needing to dominate this coupling between them. In the past, their interactions had been at Florian's whim. When Florian wanted, how Florian deemed acceptable. Hunter had allowed Florian to call all the shots and make all the decisions, and that's how he'd wound up wounded in the first place. Not anymore, though. Florian had laid his captain's hat on the bedside table next to the condoms, toys, and lube and fully embraced everything Hunter threw at him, or in this case, thrust into him.

"Oh shit, please!"

Florian had relinquished control. Had given in with wild abandon. Accepting Hunter not only into his space, but into his body. Hunter wrapped his hand in Florian's hair, tugging him up until his back was pressed to Hunter's chest. "I fucking own you now, Florian. You belong to me." Hunter came with a groan and collapsed against Florian's back.

Chapter 12

Tangled sheets were the least of Florian's worries as he lay next to Hunter catching his breath. Hunter had done exactly as he asked and owned the shit out of him. Instead of basking in the post sex euphoria doing its best to fuzz out his more rational brain, Florian couldn't help the ache in his chest that only sharpened as he thought about how to broach the next topic on Florian's list. He'd gotten Hunter to break his physical embargo, and it was time for Florian to work on rebuilding Hunter's trust in him.

"'Are we good to talk now?"

Hunter rolled over and propped his head up on his hand. "You still on that talking bullshit? I must not have done my job well enough."

"You did an outstanding job of wearing my ass out, and if that was all I wanted from you I wouldn't be talking right now."

"Then let's not talk." Hunter moved in for a kiss.

Florian allowed it, accepting his lips and tongue and reveling in the citrus and grass scent mark on Hunter's bare skin.

Mate!

Talons sprouted from Florian's fingernails, forcing Florian to pull back but not before they left thin red scratches along Hunter's shoulder. "Shit!"

"You know I love it when you get rough with me, but I never thought you'd be a scratcher." Hunter smirked and glanced over his shoulder, trying to see what stung his shoulders while Florian hid his hands beneath him.

Florian took a look at the scratches and couldn't help the relief that washed over him when he saw they weren't deep enough to leave a permanent mark. His Falcon, however, was angry Florian had blocked them from marking their mate.

"I didn't mean to mark you. I just got carried away," he rushed out.

Hunter's playful nature shifted almost immediately.

"Don't worry, Florian. I know what the deal is this time."

Florian groaned and leaned in to brush his lips against Hunter's. "No, Hunter. I, that's not what I..."

"Florian, it's fine. You don't have to remind me of where I stand with you. I know where the line is."

The dejected look on Hunter's face nearly undid Florian. He was fucking things up again.

"This isn't like last time. I fucked up by pushing you away. I have no plans of letting you go again." Florian's reassurance seemed to go in one ear and out the other.

"I just have no say at all, do I?" Hunter tried to pull away, but Florian held him firm.

Florian knew if he let Hunter retreat now, then he would have no chance at a future with him. Hunter would pull further and further away until there was nothing left of them. Just the thought sent panic through Florian's heart.

"Please, Hunt. I have no idea what it's going to take to get you to believe me when I say I want to be with you, but whatever it is, tell me and I'll do it."

Hunter sighed and looked away. "I just want the truth. I can't handle any more games with you, Florian."

"The truth? I can do that."

"You sure?"

"I told you anything," Florian said.

"Then tell me why," Hunter said.

He didn't have to elaborate. Florian knew what he was asking. Florian sat up and leaned against the headboard. Hunter sat up too, turning to face him head on with his legs crossed.

"What I'm about to tell you may be shocking and a little unbelievable, but I need you to hear me out completely before you react, okay?" Florian said.

Hunter rolled his eyes. "Quit being dramatic and get on with it. You better have a good fucking reason, too."

Florian wasn't fooled by Hunter's joking tone. He was learning that Hunter tended to joke to mask when he was feeling uncomfortable with a topic.

"I'm a Falcon Shifter," Florian said plainly and paused to see Hunter's initial reaction.

When Hunter just sat there, not betraying any emotion on his face or in his eyes, Florian had to wonder if Hunter had gotten better with his poker face in the years they'd been apart or if somehow this wasn't new information to him.

"Continue," Hunter said, waving his finger in a circular motion.

Florian frowned at the lack of teasing in Hunter's tone.

"You don't have a reaction to that?"

"So, you're done explaining? The fact you can shapeshift into a bird is why you dumped me?" Hunter's face finally cracked. His brows scrunched until his eyebrows shrunk to one thick red line, his lips thinning as he pressed them together in an unimpressed scowl.

"A Falcon, but I'm a little confused. Are you mad because you think I'm making it up or are you mad because that's not a good enough reason? It's not just that, there's more, but all related to me being a Falcon." Florian was rambling. He never rambled. Only Hunter could unnerve him so much to have him speaking before thinking.

"You really want me to answer that? Just tell me the rest."

Florian toyed with the ends of his hair, debating how to continue, all while wondering if this would be too much for Hunter.

"Have you ever heard of the term fated mate?"

"I've read a romance novel or two in my day," Hunter replied.

"I was sure there was no way you could be my fated mate. I mean, you're human, and a Cross at that. I just didn't want to lead you on, knowing one day I'd meet someone who'd make me forget you in an instant."

Hunter's gaze turned stormy. Florian leaned forward, grabbing Hunter's thigh to keep him in place. "That came out wrong. I mean, I had really strong feelings for you. I *have* really strong feelings for you."

"Yeah, I get it. You like to fuck, but you already know I'll never be your one." Hunter scooted farther away.

"No!" Florian caught Hunter by the ankle before he was fully off the bed.

"Let go, Florian," Hunter growled.

Florian didn't want to let go, and his Falcon was not having any more of his flailing attempts with their mate. The shift came over Florian before he could stop it.

"Oh shit!" Hunter jumped back as in one second Florian turned from a pleading male to a giant winged predator.

It happened so quickly, Hunter didn't get a chance to process the grotesque origami action that took place before soft feathers and sharp talons kissed his flesh.

Screech! Screech!

Hunter backed completely against the wall, trapped by the avian menace. It was one thing to know Florian was a Shifter, it was completely another to have that animal angrily screaming in your face. However, Hunter wouldn't allow Big Bird here to intimidate him. Hunter snatched a sheet off the bed and wrapped it around his waist before puffing up his chest and roaring back at the bird. *ROAR!*

The Falcon stopped screeching, and for a second, its golden rimmed eyes turned the familiar dark brown of Florian's. The bird landed on the bed and cocked its head to the side, studying Hunter.

"I believe you are a Shifter, okay? I already knew you were different. Bring Florian back now," Hunter demanded.

The bird screeched once more before its neck turned just a little too quickly. Hunter turned his gaze away, but the sickening cracks and pops almost got to him. Even when the sounds stopped, replaced with the soft whoosh of normal human breathing, Hunter was too worried to look.

"I'm back," Florian said softly.

Hunter slowly opened his eyes, and sure enough, Florian, in all his naked glory, sat in the center of the bed. Florian reached for him, his eyes pleading and almost defeated. The soft squishy part inside of Hunter that he'd thought he'd hardened against Florian was softer and squishier than ever as he climbed onto the bed and back into Florian's arms.

"You could have just told me you didn't want more. You didn't have to do what you did," Hunter said.

"I didn't do what I did to hurt you. I was trying to prove a point to myself. I didn't want to want you the way I did. I was trying to spare my own heart from breaking if I ever met the one."

"That doesn't make any sense."

"It doesn't because I had already found my one in you. I was just stupid and didn't see it until it was already too late."

Hunter brought Florian's face in line with his with a light press of his finger on Florian's chin. "You trying to say I'm your fated mate?"

Florian's shoulders relaxed as he let out a heavy breath.

"Yes, Hunter. You are my mate."

"Bullshit!"

Hunter's exclamation was exactly the reaction Florian had hoped to avoid. Did he expect Hunter to believe him right away? No. But he also hadn't expected Hunter to be so accepting of the fact he was a Shifter. Hunter had seen his bird, and despite his initial apprehension, had managed to take control of the finicky beast with an ease Florian had taken years to master. If that wasn't enough proof of their fated mate status, Florian didn't know what was. Still, Hunter obviously wasn't convinced.

"I told you it was a lot to wrap your head around," Florian said.

Hunter held up his hand in a stopping motion. "No, I get it. I just don't understand why you haven't marked me if I'm your so-called mate."

Florian opened his mouth to respond, but then Hunter's eyes went wide and grabbed his shoulder.

"You did mark me! You marked me without even asking!"

Florian put his hands up. "Hold on, I should clarify. Not everything in the novels is accurate to how things are. First, I'll admit my Falcon did try to leave a physical mark on you, but I was able to reign him in before he could. Physical marking isn't really done anymore. It can be dangerous, and extremely painful, at the very least. It's more common now to have a mating ceremony, like a human wedding. That being said, yes, I have marked you but not permanently. When we are intimate, I leave a scent mark."

"Like a dog? Wait, so that isn't just a coincidentally timed air freshener?"

"No, that's my mating scent. Every time we are together, the stronger it will be and the longer it will last. It will tell any Supernatural who you belong to."

"You're making this shit up. We've been together plenty, and while our sex is hot as fuck, the room has never smelled of anything more than leather, lube, and ass juice."

"I covered my scent mark. It's common practice for Shifters who like to keep their privacy and avoid unwanted relationships."

"Yeah, I don't need the reminder of how unwanted I was," Hunter grumbled.

"Hunt, we both know I wanted you back then, and I sure as hell want you now."

"Let's not get off topic. So, you marked me like a dog pissing on a pole, and that's somehow supposed to make me pleased as punch you've pissed all over your property." Hunter used air quotes with the word property.

"I know it's not exactly sexy, but the other option is a permanent marking like in the books. Hell, I barely kept my Falcon from marking you earlier. What I'm trying to tell you, Hunter, is what I feel for you isn't a game. I want you, Hunter. I will always want you, Hunter, and all I ask is that you try to give us another shot. A real shot at happily ever after."

"Do I even have a choice in this? You're claiming I'm your fated mate. You've already marked me." Hunter used his hands more and more as he talked, a sure sign he was becoming more agitated by the second.

Florian lunged forward and kissed Hunter to stop the tirade he knew was coming. "Hunt, you have a choice. You will always have a choice with me. If you really don't want anything to do with me. Hell, even if you only want this one weekend of fun, I will accept that. It will hurt, but I'll know it was my fault that things ended up like this."

Hunter sighed, "What do you want, Florian?"

"I want you, Hunter. I want happily ever after."

"I want to believe you, but if today highlighted anything, it was that I don't really know you."

"I'm not asking you to commit to forever right now, but maybe we can start over. Go on a real date and spend more time outside the bedroom."

"You saying you want to date me, like in public?"

"Honey, I'm taking you to dinner at my parents' tomorrow night."

"Oh, so I'm meeting the parents so soon? You do this with all the boys?"

"No, only my mate."

"Your mate? Wouldn't that require me to agree to all of this?"

Florian trailed kisses along Hunter's jawline. "If you were going to turn me down, you would have run screaming when I shifted."

Hunter moaned as Florian bent lower and laved at one of his flat nipples. "Fuck, I can't negotiate with you doing that with your tongue."

"Good. Don't think, just feel." Florian reached down to grab Hunter's thickening rod, but Hunter scooted his hips back and blocked Florian with his arms crossed over his lap.

"If we are going to do this, I want to do it right. You will introduce me as your boyfriend. We will date publicly, not just at the Wolf's Den."

"Just boyfriend?"

"I want you, Florian. I want every glittering promise of forever from you, but I can't right now. It's going to take time, and you said it yourself, you aren't proposing. We have shit to work through before we get to that point."

"I understand, however, with you wearing my neon sign of a scent mark, the Supernatural community will know you are my mate and will act accordingly."

"I don't care about that. Just don't call me mate. You're not Australian, and this isn't a scene."

"One day, you'll love it when I call you mate."

"I doubt it, but just so we're clear, I'm agreeing to date you, Flor. That is all for now."

"Perfect, but you're still meeting the parents tomorrow. If I don't bring you to dinner, they will show up sometime this weekend unannounced."

"I'll worry about that tomorrow. Tonight, let's see how much of your scent mark I can handle." Hunter uncrossed his arms and stretched his legs out alongside Florian's hips.

Florian smiled and licked his lips. "Challenge accepted."

CHAPTER 13

F lorian adjusted the buckle on his belt for the fifth time and fluffed the paisley pocket square tucked into the breast pocket of his blue sports jacket. They'd just gotten out of Florian's car in front of his parent's cabin. The lights and laughter beckoned them inside, but he was nearly sweating through his silk shirt with nerves.

"Adjust that belt buckle one more time and I'll come over there and pull it off," Hunter chuckled beside him.

Florian looked up and heat spread through his body at the sight of his mate. Dressed in the clothes he'd worn the first night they'd admitted their attraction to each other. Hunter may have been known for his casual mountain man look, but he cleaned up just as well as Florian. The reminder of that time, the heat and the passion they shared, had Florian growing hard once again, but he didn't have time to alleviate the growing ache. They were already late, since Florian had to take the long way with Hunter being human and all.

"You can undress me later. Right now, we need to get inside," Florian said, even as he made no attempt to move toward the door.

It wasn't that he didn't want Hunter to meet his parents. No, he was hesitating because he wasn't sure what Hunter's reaction would be to meeting them. Florian was the first to admit his parent's carefree lifestyle was the reason he was the man he was. Why he needed everything to be planned out in detail, all the Is dotted and the Ts crossed. The part of him that had nearly left him without his mate.

The collar of Florian's shirt suddenly felt too tight around his neck, even though the buttons were undone, exposing a generous amount of chest. More than what Florian would show for a family event, but he couldn't help watching the desire in Hunter's gaze grow with each button he'd left loose.

Hunter nudged his side. "Having second thoughts?"

Florian took Hunter's hand, lacing their fingers together. "About us? No. About exposing you to the people who gave me life?" He shrugged nervously.

"Shouldn't I be worried about that more than you?" Hunter squeezed his hand and flashed him that killer grin of his. Two rows of perfectly straight white teeth that would give any toothpaste model a run for their money, surrounded by pillow-soft lips that had massaged his dick so perfectly just a while ago. Fuck. Florian needed his parents not to ruin the small gains he'd made with Hunter this last week. If Hunter walked away from him now, Florian didn't know if he would survive it. He loved the man with everything he had. A feeling so strong he was sure he would love Hunter even if he wasn't his fated mate.

"You have nothing to worry about because I love you," Florian said, pulling Hunter closer.

"Oh, so you love me now," Hunter said flippantly.

Florian groaned and leaned in to brush his lips against Hunter's. "I love you, Hunter Cross, and I have every plan to make sure I show you how much from this day on."

"I'm sure you do," Hunter said cockily.

Part of Florian wished Hunter would say the words back, but he knew there was still more work to be done, more trust to be built in their relationship. He was okay with that for now. As long as there was hope Hunter would get to that point one day.

"I very much do," Florian said, leaning in for another kiss. Hunter met him halfway, turning what Florian had only planned to be another quick brush into something deeper. His tongue swept teasingly across Florian's lips, his hands gripping Florian's ass as his pelvis rocked into him. The fact they were late for dinner didn't matter as an electric need swept through Florian.

He had half a mind to drag Hunter into the woods and give in to the searing desire between them, but Florian caught the slight movement of the front window curtains from the corner of his eye. They had been caught, and Florian was sure his family would tease them both mercilessly for being seen so wrapped up in each other. He pressed another kiss to Hunter's lips before dragging him forward and into the house.

The smell of roast beef and potatoes filled his nostrils, and his stomach rumbled. Florian's father was in the living room with the other guests. They sat in awkward silence, and he could hear his mother snipping at Vega about her table setting skills. His dad's eyebrows met his hairline when he took in who Florian had by his side.

"Son! So glad you could finally make it."

Florian ignored the censure in his father's tone. The man hated when others were tardy, even if he had a standing rule that arriving ten minutes late was on time enough.

"We had to take the long way," was the only thing Florian offered.

In hindsight, Florian should have come by sooner and given them a pep talk about not embarrassing him in front of Hunter. It was too late now. He just hoped if anything truly outlandish were said, Hunter took it as quirky.

"Well, you're here now, and with your mate?"

Florian beamed. "Yes, sorry. Father, this is my mate, Hunter Cross. Hunter, my father, Maximus Falconer."

Hunter thankfully didn't comment on Florian's choice of words. He knew Hunter wasn't used to the endearment, but Florian wouldn't refer to him as anything else because that was what Hunter was to him. His mate, his everything.

Florian's family was cute. Hunter had come to dinner with very little expectations, but as he sat at the large oval table next to Florian, while he squirmed uncomfortably at his parents' antics, Hunter relaxed. Florian's mother chatted away about how he refused to be housebroken and had spent his childhood naked, peeing in corners or any place but a toilet. Florian's dad only smiled and occasionally tried to divert his wife with questions about Hunter's family life.

Vega was quiet through most of the dinner. Hunter noticed she kept her head down and didn't join in the conversation, not even to add to Florian's embarrassment. As far as Hunter knew, this was completely out of character from the vibrant young woman he'd come to know over the years. Vega was anything but shy.

"You're being quiet this evening, Vega. You sure you don't have any other embarrassing adventures to add?" Hunter attempted to draw her into the conversation.

Vega shrugged, "Oh, I believe Mother is doing just fine in that regard."

"I agree," Florian said and took a sip from his water glass.

It was then Florian's dad decided to ask another personal question.

"So, is it true all the Crosses live together?" he asked.

"Yes, mostly," Hunter replied.

"Mostly?"

Hunter instantly regretted leaving that easy of an opening to further pry. Sure, it was cool that Florian's dad was trying to give Florian a break from his embarrassment, but Hunter had never been good with being the topic of any conversation.

"Everyone has a place, but not all of us have stayed."

"So, when you and Florian marry, will you be okay relocating to Sullah?" Florian's mother asked, her expressive brown eyes glittering with hope for the future, and Hunter suddenly felt like the seat of his chair was covered in hot coals.

He looked to Vega for help, but she sat back and took a sip of her water. So much for their friendship. It was clear he was on his own.

"If we marry, that will be a discussion for Florian and I to have in private," Hunter replied.

"If?" Florian's mother jumped in, concern clear on her face as she looked back and forth between Florian and Hunter.

"That's enough. I brought Hunter here so you could meet him. Not for you to interrogate," Florian interjected before placing a hand over Hunter's. "If you want to leave now, I understand."

Hunter smiled and shook his head. "It's alright. Your parents are excited to see you bring someone home. I'd be more upset if it hadn't been brought up. At least now, I know they approve of me," he said, pasting on a smile.

As uncomfortable as Hunter was, he understood where Florian's parents were coming from. In fact, if it had been Hunter's family, Florian wouldn't have made it past the front door before his Aunt Melinda would have started dropping comments about how the snowcapped mountains would be the perfect backdrop for a winter wedding.

Despite Hunter's words of reassurance, Florian could see the tense set of his shoulders, the ramrod straightness of his back. Hunter was far from comfortable, and as his mate, that was unacceptable.

"Thank you for dinner, but I think it's time that we leave," Florian said and stood.

Hunter didn't move from his chair at first, but with a small tug on his hand, Hunter stood and nodded at Florian's parents.

"Thank you for a lovely dinner."

Florian's parents sat in shock as Florian pulled Hunter away from the table and out the front door.

"So, as much as I love how you got all knight in shining armor back there, I feel like I'm missing something about this whole mate business," Hunter said once they were back in his car.

All Florian wanted to do was whisk him away from his family and back to the cabin where he could work away the kinks his family had thrown into his plans to ease Hunter into things.

Still, the fact that Hunter hadn't moved his hand away from Florian's was a small sign of progress. Florian lifted Hunter's hand and pressed it to his lips.

"I should have canceled dinner," Florian muttered instead of answering Hunter's unasked question.

"We both know that isn't the problem. Your parents were fine. The issue is you are once again hiding things."

Florian scowled. He had omitted the part about rejected mate madness because he wanted Hunter to choose him. To choose to be in his life because he wanted to, not because he felt obligated by something out of both of their control.

"Being mated is more than just emotional for Shifters. It's more than just loving someone," he began.

Hunter's thumb made lazy circles on the back of his hand as if sensing just how unnerved Florian was by this conversation. "Go on, Flor. Tell me what I need to know."

"In the books you read, did it mention anything about what happens when a Shifter is rejected by their fated mate?"

"Rejection isn't exactly what romance novels are about. The Shifters were a bit over the top in the pursuit of their mates, though."

Tell him!

Florian let out a long sigh before pulling the car over. He needed to look Hunter in the eyes for what he was about to drop on him. Ideally, he should have waited until they got back to his cabin, but Hunter didn't seem like he would be much more patient with Florian.

"When a Shifter is separated from their mate, it can have devastating consequences. Not just emotional pain, but physical as well. Shifter Madness sets in, and that's dangerous for everyone."

"Dangerous, how?" Hunter sat back away from Florian, but thankfully, didn't let go of his hand.

"One of my first assignments as a Shifter enforcer was a rogue bear in the late stages of madness. His mate left him for a human, and he took it out on the first humans he came across."

Hunter pulled his hand away. "You're telling me if a Shifter's mate leaves them, they go on a murderous rampage?"

"I was just using that as an example of what could happen. It's an extreme example, and I would never let myself get to that point."

"And how would that work? You'd off yourself?"

Florian looked away. "Arrangements have been made in case."

Hunter grabbed his shoulder and pulled him back to facing him. "You're saying if I walk away from this, from you, I'm sentencing you to death?"

"You see why I didn't bring it up before? I didn't want you to feel trapped into this or obligated to stay."

Hunter closed his eyes, his cheeks visibly red, even in the low lighting of the dark car.

"Take me home, Florian," he said after a few moments of tense silence.

"Okay," Florian sighed and pulled back onto the road.

They rode in silence as Florian drove through the woods and out to the highway that would take them up the mountain and through the pass. His heart breaking with every beat, every minute, and every mile. His kept his grip tight on the steering wheel to keep from reaching over and taking Hunter's hand. To keep from veering off to one of the few scenic stops along the way to plead his case one last time. Instead, Florian let the silence continue until he parked in front of Hunter's cabin and shut off the car.

"I'm so sorry, Hunter."

"You're sorry, alright," Hunter muttered and got out of the car. Florian watched as he marched around the hood and half way to his porch before he turned around and stormed back to the car.

Florian climbed out, and when they met halfway, Hunter pulled him into his arms and kissed him. "You stupid, asshole. I should kill you myself. I will kill you myself if you do anything to make me leave you."

It took a second for Hunter's words to sink in. Florian, distracted by the kiss, was sure it was Hunter's last goodbye.

"Excuse me?"

"You heard me. Make me hate you enough to leave you, and I'll kill you myself."

"Wait, so are you not mad?"

"I'm fucking livid, but I love you, Flor. I've loved you for the last three years, and I refuse to lose you again. I'm not saying I've changed my mind about us taking things slow, but I'll be damned if..."

Florian kissed him; he didn't need to hear anything more.

EPILOGUE

Hunter took a sip of champagne and looked on in awe at the magic Vega and the Sowell Sisters Boutique had done for Mrs. Hancock's Spring Gala. Normally, a stuffy traditional affair, the English garden had been turned into a glittering fairy wonderland. Even making use of the small garden maze to surprise guests with different floral sculptures at every turn. Hunter was once again amazed by Vega's power of persuasion. The party wasn't anything Mrs. Hancock could have possibly come up with, but she beamed and chatted up anyone who would listen about how this was all her fabulous idea.

Speaking of the gracious host, she'd finally spotted him. She sashayed forward with a tall blonde on her arm.

"There you are, Hunter. I just knew you would be hiding away here somewhere," she said with a light laugh.

Hunter pasted on a smile and nodded. "Just admiring this amazing event. I do hope you sing the praises of Sowell Sisters Boutique. This is, by far, the least boring of your parties."

Her smile faltered a bit before she remembered her true objective in approaching him. She almost shoved the younger woman into Hunter.

"Hunter, I knew you would come dateless, and so, I have arranged the lovely Ms. Driscol to accompany you this evening."

Hunter didn't even bother looking at Ms. Driscol, who seemed not to care at all that she was being offered up like some sacrificial lamb. Shaking his head, Hunter took another sip of his champagne. His eyes scanned over the two women's heads until he spotted what he was searching for. Florian had been cornered by Walter Buchanon of Sowell Gate Financial. As if he knew Hunter was looking, Florian's eyes met his and his brow creased before he excused himself from the conversation.

"Ms. Driscol is the daughter of my second cousin Mildred. She went to Wharton," Mrs. Hancock continued, not at all catching on that Hunter was far from interested.

Hunter held his gaze as Florian parted the crowd between them like a man on a mission. When he was close enough, Hunter reached out to Florian and brought him flush against his side.

Mrs. Hancock paused in laying out her relative's pedigree to take note of their closeness. Her eyebrows raised so high Hunter was afraid she'd undo her Botox.

"I'm sorry. Excuse me for not properly introducing you. Mrs. Hancock, my husband Florian. Florian, this is Mrs. Hancock, our gracious host for the evening."

Her mouth fell open before she quickly regained her composure. "Oh well, I guess congratulations are in order," she said brightly, even if the look in her eyes didn't match her jovial tone.

"I guess they are," Florian said and raised his glass to toast.

Hunter clinked his glass with Florian's, not missing the question in his gaze. Hunter leaned in to whisper in his ear, "Talk about it later."

Florian and Hunter both downed their glasses. Mrs. Hancock downed her glass too, and then, not surprisingly, saw someone else she just had to introduce to Ms. Driscol. When she had disappeared into the crowd, Florian turned a stern look at Hunter.

"So, we're married now? I don't remember a ceremony," he said.

Hunter rubbed his hand up and down Florian's arm. "I thought that's what being your mate meant."

Florian smirked. "It does, but..."

"But nothing. I love you, Florian, and I want forever with you."

"Was that a proposal? Did Hunter Cross just propose?" Vega popped up out of nowhere.

"Shhh," Florian and Hunter said in unison.

Vega wrapped them both in a giant hug. "I'm so planning both ceremonies!"

"Do we get a double discount, since we're friends and family?" Florian asked.

"Hell no! Hunter can afford our new private client rate now that he's the boss man at Cross Logging," Vega snorted.

Hunter couldn't help but laugh at the angry glare Florian shot his sister.

"I'll pay you whatever you charge. I'll know it will be worth it. I only have one request," Hunter said.

"And what is that?" Vega asked.

"It's not a request for you, but for Florian."

"For me?" Florian said.

"I want you to take my name."

STELLA WILLIAMS

Stella Williams is a Blogger and USA TODAY Bestselling Paranormal Romance & Urban Fantasy Author, who lives in Washington State. She has a degree in Anthropology from The University of California, Santa Cruz. Stella prides herself in using her studies to create diverse worlds and characters for her novels. You can find more about Stella Williams on her website: www.stellawilliamsauthor.com

Also By Stella Williams

Sowell Gate Universe

Wild Cross Family

Felling Bechet

Yarding Braxton

Branding Baron

Reclaiming Hunter

Monsters & Mayhem

Peak

Unforgettable Contemporary

Unforgettable Valentine

Maura's Men Universe

Bloodlines

His Soul To Keep

To Catch Akellah
Secret of Ceres

Ferocious

Dauntless

Earnest

Zenith
Langsmith Shifters

Coy Wolf

A Night Divine

Bird of Prey
Maura's Men

Xander's Claim

Claude's Conquest

Shane's Redemption